# Laura of the Amish

Sarah Amberson

Published by Trellis Publishing, 2021.

LAURA OF THE AMISH

**First edition. July 1, 2021.**



ISBN: 979-8224492664

Written by Sarah Amberson.

# LAURA OF THE AMISH
## SARAH AMBERSON

# LAURA OF THE AMISH

Laura sighed as she spotted the rows of simple houses and farms. It had been a while since she had been at this community, nearly seven years to be exact. She had never had any intention of returning, but fate seemed to have thought otherwise.

The Amish community was in a way set apart from the rest of the ranches and farms in the area, but they were still in good distance. As the wagon drew up to her parent's house, her gaze drifted over to a modern ranch house only across the field from the familiar front yard.

That farm hadn't been there before, but she shouldn't be surprised, many things were bound to have changed in the time she had been away.

There was something else that had changed but it wasn't with her childhood town. She glanced down beside her at her six year old daughter.

She hadn't been alive when Laura had last been here, and Laura could only hope that her past community would accept them the way they had said they would.

Despite her father's kind words and reassurances, Laura was skeptical. she knew that the Amish were known for many things, and one of them was not being overly accepting of outsiders, even if they had been family once upon a time.

Laura knew that she would be considered an outsider, and even after she made the vows to the church, she was sure that it would continue for quite some time to some degree.

Even though she had never broken a vow, but had simply left before she made one, it didn't make her much more accepted in the eyes of the Amish. She would forever be soiled in their eyes.

She let out another sigh. If she had any other choice she would be as far away from this community as possible, but as much as she had come to accept outside life, she could never accept the options that she had as a young single mother left to fend for herself in the Wild West.

She had tried it for the last six months, and it hadn't worked out well. She had cleaned houses, taught in the schoolhouse, and worked every other odd but respectable job out there, but the truth was, there wasn't enough opportunity, and she had nowhere to leave her young daughter that she felt comfortable with.

She fought the tears that welled up in her eyes. Her husband's death had been unexpected. Like so many others, they had made plans to live with each other and create a family for years to come until they'd died of old age.

Unfortunately, that hadn't worked out either, and now Laura had to come back to the one place she had worked so hard to forget that it existed. It wasn't that she didn't have some good memories from the Amish community. There were nice things, the way they fellowshipped together, her friends who had always been there for her, the love that her parents had shown her.

But little by little, Laura had seen the side of the Amish that wasn't so warm or friendly. The way people excommunicated their own children, the way she and her friends were forced to never talk to one of their closest friends until they repented. It was a side that you couldn't truly understand until you saw it and Laura had seen it too many times.

When she had been seventeen, she had needed to make a decision on whether or not she wanted to join the church. Laura knew that if she joined the church and then left, she would never be able to see or speak to her family as long as they remained within the church.

She had chosen the only option that would allow her to one day speak to them again and that was never making a vow in the first place. It wasn't that she had planned to stick around, but there was some part of her that couldn't come to terms with never seeing her family again.

She thanked her younger self for that decision now. She knew that it was selfish and in a way it was to benefit herself, but she didn't know what else they had expected her to do.

Her father had insisted that there was no problem bringing her daughter, Katie back the community, In fact he had insisted that it would be good for her young daughter's growth.

As Laura stared into her daughter's deep brown eyes, she wasn't so sure. Could she risk putting Katie through what she had gone through when she was young?

What if one day Katie decided to go against the church and she was unable to speak to her, or eat with her? The thought made Laura shiver.

She had been seriously considering taking the vow. She knew that it was most likely the only way her parents would allow them to stay for any length of time, but she wasn't sure yet whether she could commit to this way of life.

Her father had reassured her that the church had changed in the last seven years, but Laura needed to see it for herself.

She squared her shoulders as she leapt from the wagon and helped her daughter down beside her. It was time to see them again.

She loved her parents and had spent many a night crying herself to sleep, not knowing if she could go through with what she was doing. But somehow she had found the strength. She knew if she saw her parents often, they would convince her to come back.

Even at seventeen, she had known the only way to leave this community for good was to leave and never look back. That was until now.

Her mother and father stood on the simple white porch, their smiles wide as they waited for Laura and Katie to approach.

Laura sucked in a breath as she realized how much older they looked. They both had the beginnings of grey hair and her mother had a tired look on her face.

She looked around the farm for her siblings. She missed them too, her three older brothers and her two younger sisters. She didn't know if all of them were still here. If she had left, it was most probably that at least one other from the family had left too. That was what the church taught anyway, that rebellion in a family spread like disease.

She wasn't sure if this was true or not. Did it really have to be the fault of the first person to leave that the others followed? Maybe the bravery of the first one helped them act on thoughts they already had. Either way, whether it was their fault or not, there was no arguing with the church. What they said was truth and anyone who questioned that would be punished.

"Laura..." Her mother's voice was full of emotion that made Laura's already teary eyes nearly spill over. She had missed her mother the most and thought of her often. While Laura had never really been shunned, she had always thought that if she was, it would be her mother who talked to her. Now that she had a daughter of her own, she was sure of it.

She had heard of people that talked to those who were excommunicated in the church. They often were shunned themselves and it was something that very few were willing to risk for one another, but a mothers love, well there was nothing stronger than that.

Laura couldn't bring herself to say anything but instead let herself relax into her mother's embrace. The smell of freshly baked bread filled her nostrils and memories came rushing back; running barefoot in the yard as the women prepared a picnic of delicious foods for them to eat, talking with her friends under the huge tree that still stood nearby. The tree seemed smaller than she remembered it, but then again, she had been a little shorter and had seen things differently as a child.

Her father surprised her by giving her a warm embrace. Laura found herself enjoying it and having some memories of him flash back as well. Her father had always been a good father, despite being strict and one of the many reasons she had decided to leave and never come back. He had never been cruel to her.

"Your brothers wanted to be here, but we thought it best if we greeted you first," he said in his gruff voice.

Laura knew what that meant, her parents wanted to make sure she wouldn't be a further bad influence on the family than she had already been. She had kept this in mind when they had come, she had dressed herself and her daughter in appropriate attire, in line with the Amish expectations.

They weren't too different from the clothes of the typical western women, except that Amish preferred plain colors and plain patterns. Laura had made her dress as well as her daughters dress. There were some things from the Amish days that she had never forgotten.

"I'm so glad you are home," Laura's mother said, and she could tell from the look in her eyes that her joy was genuine.

Laura watched as her father went into another room, he was most likely going to get the Bible or a reminder of the rules. She still knew them by heart but she wasn't about to offend her father only moments after returning.

"Your brother and sister will be happy to see you to," Laura's mother looked away slightly as she referred to Laura's siblings.

"Are they the only ones who haven't married yet?" Laura didn't' want to ask outright but it was clear by the sadness in her mother's eyes that she knew what Laura wanted to know.

"Your two older brothers, and Elise, well they left soon after you did." Her mother gave a sigh but replaced her sad look with a neutral one when Laura's father came back.

Laura felt a wave of guilt wash through her. She knew that both of her older brothers had made vows to the church. They had simply left their community and their church. In her parents eyes, they no longer existed.

As she watched her mother a little closer, she had to wonder if she had told her about her siblings to keep her from slipping up and talking about them or if she had done so because she wanted an excuse to talk about them.

She looked back at her daughter once more. If it was her, Laura knew she couldn't do it. She couldn't stay in the community while her daughter was sent away, never to be spoken to or of again. Her heart broke for her mother. She couldn't imagine what kind of pain she was going through having three of her children still out of her life.

Even worse, she hated to think of the pain she herself had caused her.

"Okay everyone, we have some things to discuss so let's sit at the table." Laura could tell that her father was trying to sound cheerful. Laura gripped Katie's hand tightly as they sat down. She needed to be here for her daughter, she needed to be strong for her daughter.

She plastered a smile on her face and sat up straight. This wasn't the first time she had been sat at this table for a talk and she had a feeling it wouldn't be the last time.

As her father went over the rules she could feel Katie getting drowsy at her side. She could feel the disapproving gazes of her parents on her small daughter leaning up against her, falling into sleep.

She knew that she hadn't been as strict as her parents, but for her there were other things she considered more important and at this moment she was pretty sure her parents wouldn't say anything about Katie's misbehavior.

She put her arm around her daughter and let her sleep, if she felt anything like Laura did, she was truly exhausted.

Eventually it was time for dinner and Laura found herself appreciating the delicious food she remembered so well.

After dinner, Laura tucked Katie into bed and then slipped outside the house for a walk. She needed some air.

—-*—-

Mark breathed in the cool night air. He always walked his fence line before bed. It was more of a habit than anything now. At first it had been to make sure that there was nothing amiss. He couldn't be blamed for not trusting people in a new place, but now it was just because he enjoyed the little ritual he had created for himself.

As he approached the part of the fence that met up with his Amish neighbors, he was surprised to see a young woman leaning up against the wooden planks.

She looked deep in thought and it was hard to tell by the dusk light, but he was pretty sure he had never seen her before. This was odd for him because he had done business or traded with nearly every Amish family in the community and knew everyone, even the women of the family.

"Good evening," he said as quietly as he could. Despite his effort, the young woman jumped a little and searched around. After a few moments, her eyes found his.

Mark felt himself become momentarily stunned. The girl was definitely someone he had never seen before.

Her wavy black hair was pulled back at her neck, an unusual style for the Amish, and her face was beautiful in a simple way that Mark was sure he couldn't explain even if he tried.

"Good evening," the young woman said, then stared at him as if waiting for him to continue the conversation.

"I was just checking my fence line. I didn't mean to startle you," Mark explained, motioning to the long fence that spanned his property.

"Oh, I'm sorry, I didn't know it was your fence... I just needed a breath of air and came out here and it looked like a good a spot as any." The young woman looked back at the house as if she were worried about something.

"It's no trouble. Are you new here? I don't reckon I've ever seen you before," Mark asked curiously, placing his elbows on the fence but being careful to keep a certain distance from the young woman. He knew how the Amish could be and he was surprised the young woman had talked to him at all.

"Yes, and no," the girl replied with a laugh that was as enticing as everything else about her.

"I actually grew up here, but I left seven years ago and just came back now," she explained with a sigh. Even in the dim light, Mark could see the shadows that filled the young woman's eyes.

There was something troubling her that she wasn't saying.

"Not exactly the welcome home party you expected?" he asked with a small sympathetic smile.

"It was fine," Laura said her lips tightening. "I expected it wouldn't go great coming back to everything I left behind and with a daughter on top of that," she said wistfully.

"You have a daughter?" Mark hadn't meant for the question to sound so judgmental. This young woman was a mystery that seemed to get deeper with every detail he learned.

"I should go." The young woman pushed herself off the fence and turned back towards the house.

"Sure, I'll see you around...umm..." Mark paused. He still didn't' know the woman's name.

"Laura," she said softly.

"I'm Mark and it was nice to meet you," he said with a wave. He watched Laura disappear into the darkness as she slipped back to her house.

There was something about her that intrigued Mark, and that was saying something. He had started his ranch here five years ago, and in that time, he had learned that while the Amish were great for doing business with, it was best if you kept your distance when possible.

They tolerated outsiders, saw them as people that they had to deal with, but it seemed that they had a hard time becoming friends with them.

This particular Amish church did allow friendships, and because of this, there were a few men in the Amish community that might make it unto Mark's list of friends.

But real loyal friendship with the Amish, was impossible. You had to know that any little disagreement with the church and you would be shunned.

Yes, they didn't exactly have that written in, shunning specific outsiders, but Mark had seen it.

If you got on their bad side, they would coordinate to make you feel it, regardless if you were Amish or not. It was for this reason that Mark kept his distance. He couldn't bring himself to put his ranch in jeopardy. He needed nice neighbors and so far, that's all the Amish had been to him.

He whistled a little tune as he retreated back to his ranch house. It was lonely sometimes, living on the ranch all alone. His only company were the ranch hands he hired on occasion to help him with the big things, and his dog. That was one benefit of living with the Amish. They made great workers when you needed them.

He sat himself down at a small desk in his parlor. He had prepared the desk himself, for writing letters back home.

That was one thing that he diligently did, no matter what. He knew that his parents wouldn't be around forever. It was his hope that one day they would gather the courage they needed to follow him out here to the west and live with him, but so far, they hadn't seemed sure about the idea.

He let his pen touch his paper and his thoughts began to flow,

*Hello Ma and Pa,*

He told them about the new calf that was in his barn and he told them about his recent struggles with crops. Surprisingly towards the end he found himself writing about the mysterious Amish woman he'd met.

As he added finishing touches, he couldn't help but smile. He could already imagine all the warnings his mother would be sending his way.

But they didn't have to worry, all he was interested in was a friendship, a simple friendship just like he had with the rest of the community, wasn't he?

Laura hummed a little tune as she hung the clothes out to dry. She tried to cheer herself up with the singing, but she kept it quietly to herself as she knew that singing songs outside of the hymn book was strictly forbidden.

It had been nearly three weeks since they had returned to the Amish and she was surprised at how well it had gone up until now. She did realize that the pressure to take the vow to the church was growing. Her father had been mentioning it nearly every day and the bishop had been to visit her twice already.

They had a plan that Laura certainly wasn't happy about. They had chosen a man that would make a good husband for her. The man already had had a wife who had died two years ago, and she had left two young boys behind.

Laura felt trapped by their suggestion. She had come back out of necessity, nothing more and would take the church vow if she had to, but marrying and becoming a mother of two more small children and a wife to a man she didn't love, were not part of what she had signed up for.

She sighed sadly, if she turned them down, she risked putting what she had built in jeopardy. But if she accepted, she would be miserable the rest of her life most certainly. She had never pictured herself married to an Amish man and she couldn't wrap her mind around it. He would be the Lord of her life other than God and she would be bound to obey him in everything.

"Why such a serious face?" Mark's voice made her start. He had a habit of doing that; sneaking up on her.

Laura had done everything, even being completely rude to him, to show him that she wasn't interested in getting to know him or even talking with him.

If her parents found out how much she had already talked with him, that could be cause enough for them to demand she marry immediately.

She couldn't think of anything worse. At least up until now she had done nothing wrong, so she had given them no reason to demand any rash action from her. They were giving her space, time to adjust to her new life.

The thing was, the more Mark tried to get into her life, the more she enjoyed his company.

It was nice to have contact with someone who wasn't part of the community. He seemed to be a kind person who actually understood the life she had led for the last seven years.

"I'm not serious," Laura said softly, though she knew that she wasn't convincing anyone.

"You can't fool me. I think I know you better than that," Mark said with a little chuckle making Laura blush.

"We've only spoken a few times. You don't know me at all," Laura said a little too sharply.

She couldn't be seen being friendly with Mark. She just couldn't.

"Well, I actually am quite observant," Mark said with a mischievous glint in his eye.

"Where's your daughter?" Mark searched around her toward the house. "You know that they can't see this side of the house from the windows," Mark said, lowering his voice.

Laura pretended not to care but her shoulders relaxed a little at his words. She hadn't really been thinking about that but hearing him admit that he knew what she was worried about put her at ease somehow.

"My daughter is out playing in front," Laura said trying to change the conversation.

"So I heard a rumor you were going to get married." Mark's words caused Laura to freeze in her tracks. How was there already a rumor about it when she had barely heard herself?

"Actually, they want me to marry a man in the community, but I have not agreed to marry him, nor do I intend to." Tears prickled Laura's eyes as she hung another piece of clothing.

She had a feeling that she was going to be pushed into this marriage whether she liked it or not. She considered fleeing back to a different town, but the thought filled her with fear. She had a daughter to look after. It wasn't that simple. Laura knew that everything she did would affect another part of her life and not only that, it would affect her daughter.

"Well, you should tell your future husband that, because he has been spreading it around as if you'd already accepted," Mark said with a serious look that was rare for him.

"Why do you care?" Laura asked suddenly in an attempt to remove the attention from herself.

"Oh, I don't, but I thought you might, seeing as you're the one who's supposed to get married and all." Mark paused and for some reason Laura found herself speaking.

"They're not really going to give me a choice, are they?" Laura said, her voice wavering for a moment.

"You know, from what I've seen, if you stay long enough, you'll end up doing whatever it is they want you to do," Mark said, and Laura could see true sympathy in his eyes.

Whatever Mark said, in that moment, she could see that he did care and it made her feel just a little bit better.

"I don't' want to marry him. I don't even know the man, but I have a daughter to think about. If I left, where would I go? How would I support myself? You know as well as anyone what kind of steady work there is for women out here in the west and it isn't respectable," Laura said a tear falling unto her cheek.

She had finished hanging the clothes now and was standing there, spilling her fears and thoughts to Mark for what reason, she had no idea.

Mark reached out quickly and wiped the tear away from her cheek. His hand was rough against her skin but it was kind, comforting.

"You know, sometimes when you really start looking, you will find solutions right in front of you," he said in a low voice.

"I am looking, I just haven't found anything," Laura said, her voice full of emotion as she stared up into the eyes of the one person who had been truly kind from his heart to her since she had gotten here.

"Keep looking Laura. Don't give up. Don't do something that your heart tells you is wrong for you." With those words, Mark was off towards the fence and disappearing over it. Not moments later, Laura's mother joined her out by the line.

Laura went through the motions of being present the rest of the day, but she couldn't get her mind off of what mark had said to her. Maybe there was something that she was missing. If there was, she was determined to find it.

Mark watched Laura and her mother from afar. He hated seeing her so sad. It was something that such a beautiful young woman shouldn't have to experience, being forced to do things against her will to protect her child.

He had only known Laura for a few short weeks and in that time had only been able to get close enough to talk to her a few times, but those times that he did had made him more attached than he would have liked to be.

He was developing feelings for Laura and he scolded himself against it. It was the one thing he had promised himself never to do; fall in love with an Amish woman.

Determining to leave Laura to her own fate and solutions, he set about his work. He couldn't let this young woman's issues destroy the work he had done so far on his farm.

—-*—-

Rain pelted down on Mark and everything around him. He was trying to get all the livestock in the barn.

The storm had surprised him, and by the looks of things, it had surprised his neighbors as well.

He could see Laura struggling to get the milk cow in the barn. Despite only only one day and a half passing since he had promised to stay away from her, he hurried over the fence to help her.

If anyone had a problem with it, they shouldn't. It was just shameful that no one was helping her themselves. Letting a woman do this all on her own was just inconsiderate.

"Where's your family?" Mark yelled above the wind.

"They went into town. My mother got sick and I had to stay behind to take care of the animals because the storm was just starting," Laura yelled back.

The two of them worked in silence, putting in all the cows and horses until each animal was in their proper dry place out of the storm.

"Thank you for your help," Laura said gently as they stood at the door way of her house.

"It's no problem," Mark said, shifting uneasily on his heels.

"I'd invite you in, except you know how my parents are. I'm not sure they'd think it was proper," Laura said with a little chuckle.

"No, no problem. I understand." The rain was letting up now, as if its earlier vigor had all been a joke to make them run and scurry to put the animals away.

"You can take my umbrella and I will get it tomorrow," she said.

She reached for the umbrella that she had left by the door and Mark jumped forward to get it at the same moment. His hand wrapped around it just as Laura's did and they found themselves holding hands.

Mark didn't release her hand and she didn't pull away. They stood like that, looking into each other's eyes for a second, and that second was one second too long.

"Laura, what do you think you are doing?" the angry voice caused both of them to jump equally as the door burst open.

Her mother gasped audibly.

Laura opened and closed her mouth, at a loss of words as how to explain their blunder that had lasted just a second too long.

"Let me explain sir," Mark said also scrambling for a way to explain what Laura's father had just seen.

As he turned, his heart sank. Beside Laura's parents, stood the bishop, and the look on his face was anything but friendly.

"There is nothing to explain. You should be going now," her father growled. Her father's voice was as cold as steel and Mark almost found himself afraid of him, but he was more afraid for Laura who had the frightened look of a mouse caught by the cat. She was a as pale as a sheet and stood with her hands clasped together, her knuckles pale with strain.

"You're right. Good day, ma'am," Mark said, addressing Laura hoping that she could see the extreme sympathy he had in his eyes. He wished that he could whisk her away with him so she wouldn't have to deal with her angry father, the angry bishop, or her mother who looked devastated.

But Mark knew that Amish would deal with things the Amish way and for now that was who Laura had chosen to be Amish.

With a heavy heart, Mark trudged through the mud and the remaining drizzle back to his ranch. He would keep an eye out for the opportunity to talk to Laura soon. For now, all he could do was hope they were lenient with her.

—-*—-

Laura sat in dread at the kitchen table. It was funny how a simple table could have such wonderful and such terrible memories all at the same time. It was the one place that both things happened in equal measure.

"Do you know how this reflects on the church, on the community?" The bishop was talking too loudly, and his voice scraped against Laura's nerves. She hadn't been listening to whatever he had said before that but had been focusing on the intricate little patterns on the wood of the table.

This question though, was too bold to ignore so she nodded her head in what she hoped was a complacent way.

The truth was, she didn't think she had held Mark's hand for more than a second and the electricity that had shot through her as their hands had touched was something she hadn't felt since her husband and she had met.

"Father, may I speak?" she inquired with as much respect as she could muster.

"There is nothing to say!" he said angrily. You had no business bringing a man into the house at all and certainly no business having personal contact with him! You may have become accustomed to that sort of behavior when living with the Englishmen, but it will not be tolerated here. Do you understand?" he thundered.

"Yes Father," was all she could say.

"After everything we've done for you, the kindness we've shown you in taking you back!" Her father was yelling now, and Laura watched as her mother shrunk back into her chair with sadness. His hand slapped down on the table with emphasis and she and her mother jumped in unison.

She knew what was coming, the ultimatum hat would cause Laura to stay or leave, and most likely her mother thought she would choose the latter. After all, wasn't that what she had always done? She desperately didn't want to cause her mother more pain, but she couldn't imagine putting herself in a situation that was so oppressive either.

"I am sorry to have to do this, but you give me no choice!" Laura's father had stopped pacing and now stood directly in front of Laura.

Laura could see the way that his eyes were full of fire and his beard quivered from his effort to control himself. She looked down momentarily and he jerked her chin upward forcing her to look into his eyes again.

"You *will* marry the man we have chosen for you and take a vow to the church the day after tomorrow. Otherwise, we will have no choice but to shun you and you will be dead to us."

With that Laura's father left the room leaving a dark stillness behind. After a few moments, realizing there was nothing more he could say, the bishop left as well.

"Oh Laura," was all her mother could say and Laura couldn't find any words that described how she was feeling.

She had messed up, and now she would have to decide. Her heart broke at the thought. She felt as if she had to choose between prison and a desert island.

She held her mother's hand and let the tears flow down her cheeks. What could she do now?

—-*—-

Mark hadn't heard from Laura the rest of the day and he had grown quite worried, but he also didn't dare walk over to the Amish house and ask what had happened, so he waited and watched her yard, but saw nothing.

After dusk he was surprised to hear a timid knock on his door. He hurried to open it and was even more surprised to find Laura, looking shaken and upset, standing there.

"What's happened? Are you all right? I'm so sorry, I didn't mean to..." Mark trailed off. He had meant to and they both knew it. There was truly nothing he could say to mend the situation.

"They're going to make me marry him," Laura sobbed, tears streaming down her cheeks.

Mark felt anger rise within him and suddenly he realized that he couldn't stand the thought of Laura marrying some man against her will. He also hated to think what it would be like not to see Laura out in her yard or chat with her at night when she came to the fence for a breath of fresh air.

"Then don't," Mark said huskily, taking a quick step towards her. He gathered her hands up into his and stared down into her beautiful face.

"Marry me instead. I've come to care for you Laura. I know we haven't known each other long, but I want to marry you. Become my wife. I will do my best to make you happy," he added.

"I have a daughter," Laura said in a whisper.

Mark chuckled. He couldn't have forgotten if he had wanted to.

"It's okay, I've always wanted children, the more the merrier," Mark said with a soft laugh. I will treat her as my own.

"I know that we will still be close to your parents and they won't probably be friendly to you for a couple years. But at least you'll be able to see them from afar, and you will be happier with me, I promise. You don't belong Amish, you just don't." There wasn't anything else Mark could think of to convince Laura and he waited impatiently for her to answer.

Finally after several moments of agonizing silence, she nodded her head.

"I'll marry you Mark. You're right, I don't belong to the Amish anymore. And we'll figure it out, day by day," she added, trying to smile through her tears.

Mark didn't wait another moment to wrap Laura into his arms. Despite all the trouble their union would bring, he had never felt happier about anything in his entire life.

# The Amish Promise

## MEGHAN MASON

Nothing could have created a more romantic and joyful afternoon, as David and Rachael sat upon the checked picnic blanket. David had been planning this occasion for months now, and he had put very careful preparations into what was hopefully going to prove to be the happiest days of their lives. David had fallen in love with Rachael from the beginning, when they first met at the Amish community fall social. Very soon after, he knew that she was exactly perfect for him in every way possible. He wanted her to be his wife, and to build a family together. Because of this happy realization, David had been making plans about how and when to pop the important question. He had secretly already asked her father, Abel, for his daughter's hand in marriage, and Abel had been pleased to hear of David's intentions. He knew David to be a very hardworking young man who respected the traditions of the Amish with much reverence. He could not have chosen a better husband for Rachael if he had tried. David left her father's barn that day, his heart bursting with pride and happiness. Now his biggest responsibility was to create the perfect atmosphere to ask his beloved to marry him.

It had taken David just two weeks to imagine the plan, and put it into action! He wanted something simple, so he opted for a lovely picnic lunch in the meadow of his parents' farm. It was situated nicely in the back of the property, and was filled with large, mature oak trees, wildflowers in full bloom, and warm yet breezy weather. He enlisted the help of his eldest sister, Gloria, to assist him in making a light lunch. She had prepared sandwiches, fresh fruit, and homemade apple cider, and packed it all away in a wicker picnic basket. David selected a soft blanket, and went off to pick up Rachael, for what she thought to be a simple date in the fresh air.

Once there, David laid out blanket his grandmother had made years ago, and guided Rachael by the hand to sit down for lunch. His heart soared as he admired his true love, and it felt like all Gott's creatures understood what was about to happen. Birds tweeted from their nests, bugs stayed conveniently away, and the few rabbits and squirrels looked on as if excited to see the plan play out. David withdrew a tiny wooden box from his breast pocket, and looked her straight in the eyes,

"Rachael, you must know by now that you are my beloved. I want to ask for you to become my wife," and he opened the box to reveal a simple golden band, "please say yes, and make me the happiest man alive," he declared. Rachael's glistening eyes gleamed in the sunlight, as she gazed at the glint of the beautiful band, and she instantly knew what her answer was to be,

"Yes, David! I thought you'd never ask," she laughed, and he slipped the band onto her finger. They were far too excited to eat any lunch, so they hastily packed up the basket, and returned to the farmhouse. There, as was to be expected, sat his mamm, daed, schwesters and bruders,

"What is this now?" asked his daed, "back so early from the meadow?"

"Yes, father! Rachael had said yes to my proposal, though we were too excited to even eat," and he looked at Gloria to make sure he had not inadvertently hurt her feelings. Gloria giggled, and exclaimed in Pennsylvania Dutch,

"Nau is awwer bsll Zert!" which translated into English as *Now it's about time!* Everyone congratulated the young couple, and the basket was re-opened to share amongst the family. Gloria had made lots of extra anyway, so it turned into quite a nice family gathering.

It was beginning to darken as the evening set in, and David drove Rachael back to her home in the buggy. They said their goodbyes, and promised to meet soon, after the big harvest. All the men, including her own father and bruders would be working hard to harvest all the grain, corn, and other seasonal crops. After that big job, the two would certainly have plenty of time to plan the ceremony. She waved at David, as he steered the old buggy back towards his father's farm.

Rachael told her family all about the amazing afternoon that she had spent with David's family, and showed off the pretty band. It would not be long before they were joined together in matrimony. Her mamm cried, as mamms are prone to do, and ran to get the family wedding dress out of the hope chest in her room. It had been in their family for generations, and her mother was overjoyed that her only daughter was now going to be the special girl to wear the dress. Though made of simple cotton with spots of delicate embroidery, it was such a meaningful family tradition. She began to daydream of perhaps having a granddaughter someday that the dress would be passed on to eventually. Her own sister had never married, and had recently taken ill in an Amish settlement in Indiana, so the dress had passed to Ellen instead. Poor Eliza had had no children of her own, and though she felt sad for her sister, she was happy to be next in line for the dress. The rest of the evening was spent eating a celebratory supper of roast beef, roasted potatoes, and the green beans picked fresh from the garden. It appeared that nothing could ruin the joy of these families that were about to become one!

Early the next morning, while Rachael was picking vegetables from the garden, a stranger in a buggy came rumbling up the drive towards their home. The man removed his hat in polite greeting to Rachael, and went to knock upon the door. Her mamm answered, as the menfolk were out for the harvest work, and the girls were all home keeping up with the household chores. Her mamm seemed to recognize the stranger, and invited him in to the house. Rachael was curious about who the stranger could be. The Amish rarely had unknown visitors outside of the community, so this was slightly intriguing, if not a bit unsettling. If Rachael had only known just how unsettling the stranger's news was to be, she would probably have run off that very minute towards David's family. Her mamm called her in with a grim look about her face, and it was then that her heart sank. She felt an unnerving feeling of unexplainable dread, as she made her way from the garden to the house. Why was this man here, and why had she been beckoned by her mamm? Many anxious questions began to form in her mind, as she plodded carefully with her apron full of vegetables. Mamm took the vegetables, and bade her daughter to sit down at the family table. She did not look happy, and this further worried Rachael,

"Daughter, something dreadful has happened to your aunt Eliza. This is Brant, come all the way from Indiana to explain the details." She looked at her daughter with pity and sadness, but Rachael was still clueless as to how this should involve her. She listened to Brant's words,

"Hello, my dear. I am Brant Williams. I am an old friend of your mamm's family, and I have traveled very far to deliver some saddening news. Your Aunt Eliza's health is now worse than ever, and a family member is needed to come care for her in her dying days." Rachael's face fell at this news, as she barely knew her Aunt Eliza, and had a terrible feeling she was to be that family representative,

"What is it that must be done for auntie?" she said hesitantly.

Her mamm took hold of the situation, and explained,

"Rachael, dear, you are the not the eldest child, as your bruder, Hamm, is over twenty, but as the oldest female, you are expected to go and care for Eliza. I would gladly take your place, but the responsibility falls to you."

"What does this all mean? What will happen now that I am to marry David?" she inquired desperately, "I am to be planning a wedding in two short weeks, mamm!" Her mother's countenance turned stern, and Rachael knew then that she had spoken with selfishness. If this was truly her duty, she was bound to do whatever was necessary for Aunt Eliza. This would undoubtedly mean many months away from home, and from David. She tried in vain to hide her tears, but only could squeak out a few words before fleeing to her bedroom,

"Sorry, Mr. Williams an mamm. I, of course, will go," and she dashed away towards the back of the house. She threw herself pathetically on the bed, and let out all the tears that came with the disappointment of postponing the wedding. All had been so happy the night before, and now it felt like the world was coming to an end. Little did Rachael know what tragic events were about to unfold in her otherwise ordinary, simple, and predictable life in the quaint community of Oakhurst Village.

The following afternoon, Rachael was packed and ready as she ever could manage to be, and Mr. Brant Williams had stayed the night to give Rachael more time to let the news soak in. He had his own family, after all, and knew quite well the sacrifices that were sometimes required. Still, he felt badly for Rachael, knowing the predicament caring for Eliza now meant. Her wedding would be postponed, but he and her parents encouraged her to keep the faith that all would work out in good time. She sent word to David via one of her bruders, and received a reply that wished her well, though expressed his sorrow that they would have to alter their plans. Both knew in their hearts, however, that if someone was in need, it was the right thing to do. Brant hooked up the horses to the rickety looking buggy for their rather long trip to Indiana. They would stop along the way to spend the nights at various Amish villages, and Brant reassured her parents that she would be well taken care of throughout the journey. It was also explained to her that Eliza was in a bad way, close to death, and would require ongoing care until Gott called her home to his heavenly paradise. The doctor would come and assess Eliza once again once Rachael had arrived. It appeared that all was well in hand, and that caring for her aunt would be a good and kind gesture. After all, she was family, and no one should have to suffer alone or so far from family if it could be prevented. She prayed about her new adventure in Indiana, a place she'd never been, and asked Gott to bless Eliza. She could not bear it if she was to suffer in unbearable pain, and was not all that familiar with medical care. Her mamm had given her a book of household remedies, and instructed her to make use of it if needed. She held tightly to the book as if it was the guidebook for caring for the dying, even though Eliza was most likely too far gone to be aided by homemade health recipes. They would have to rely on the doctor's orders, and try to make Aunt Eliza as comfortable as possible. It was also understood that Brant would drop in weekly to deliver groceries and supplies, so that Rachael's full attention could be on her aunt's welfare. Eliza owned a small cottage in the main street of her village. She had many friends, but it being harvest, the women of their houses would be needed at home. Rachael was the best option, and she resolved to do her best with a compassionate and loving heart. She tried to pass the long journey by imagining life as David's wife, and the bopplis they might have one day soon.

After a week's journey, Brant and Rachael arrived in Well's Landing. If she never saw the seat of that old buggy again, it would be too soon. Gingerly, she stepped down as Brant helped her down. He took charge of her modest traveling bag, and they proceeded to call upon Aunt Eliza. There was a friendly nurse assistant currently sitting at her bedside keeping diligent watch. She offered Rachael advice as to how to comfort her ailing relative until Doc Warner could make the drive into the center of town. Apparently, the doctor was to be expected the day after tomorrow, so hopefully Rachael could handle things until then. With a grateful hug, Rachael bid Brant and the nurse assistant goodbye, and began to settle in to her small room beside her aunt's main bedroom. It was a connecting room, with a shared indoor bathroom, so at least there would be that convenience. The nurse had left instructions on when to brew the medicinal tea, and what times to try to feed broth to Eliza. Rachael had to admit that the unfortunate woman whom she barely knew, looked like she had been ravished by disease for some time now. She unpacked her bag, and went off to the kitchen to boil some water.

Doc Warner made his appearance at noon the following day. He took all of Eliza's vital signs, and asked Rachael to please continue the same care for as long as Eliza would last. If her aunt experienced any adverse reactions or serious pain, she was to send word as quickly as possible. He directed her to run next door to the general store where they had a modern phone installed. That way, the doctor would be there in good time with something to ease the pain or increased sickness. Rachael followed him out, thanked him, and paid the bill with the money her mamm had sent for that purpose. She then returned to Eliza's bedside, where her aunt mostly slept. During these lengthy naps, Rachael wrote daily letters home to David, and worked on sewing their wedding quilt. In the evenings, she straightened the tiny house, and prepared broth and tea, in addition to her own small meals. She always had David on her mind, and hoped all was going well back home with the harvesting. She always mentioned in the letters how much she missed her fiancé, and that she hoped that Eliza would not have to endure too much more suffering. It was difficult for Rachael to comfort her when she was awake, as she could never get comfortable. During these lucid times, she read aloud to Aunt Eliza from the bible.

The following week, she received a letter from home, but this time it looked like it had been written in David's mother's hand. She wondered why the letter was addressed in Mrs. Todd's handwriting rather than David's, but she was excited to get the letter nonetheless. She carefully opened the envelope, and perused the contents of the letter. Rachael felt faint as she read the horrible news about David! His mamm reported that during the past week, a terrible accident had befallen her son. During an afternoon of harvesting with his daed and bruders, David had been asked to go fetch some feed from the barn. The feed sacks had been stored up above in the hay loft area. As David climbed the ladder to the loft, the top rung broke in half, causing him to fall to the barn floor. He had broken both legs, and cracked several ribs. The doctor came at once, but David was in serious pain. In addition to the broken bones, he apparently suffered a damaging blow to the head. Upon landing awkwardly on the barn floor, he had hit the side of his head on a large tool box. The head injury was proving to be the most serious of David's injuries, and he had fallen into a state of unconsciousness shortly after the doctor had left. Mrs. Todd went on to explain that they called the doctor back as soon as possible, but that he was rather skeptical that David would awaken given the severity of the fall. He had sustained so many injuries that the family was growing fearful of his recovery. Rachael dropped the letter, and slumped to the floor. How could this be happening? Her David was hurt, and she was so far away. It was heartbreaking news, and she sobbed much of the night. Not only was she going to lose her aunt, but the love of her life was now clinging to life, and she was not able to get frequent updates. A letter per week was all that was coming in, and she continued to cry herself to sleep every night. Every letter conveyed similar news that David was not showing any improvement. He was still deep in a coma, and his schwesters and mamm were keeping a very close eye on him. To make matters worse, poor Aunt Eliza had taken a turn for the worse, and was now becoming delirious, murmuring in her sleep, and raving when she was awake. She phoned Doc Warner, and he prescribed a sedative from the chemist. An errand boy delivered the powder to the door with instructions on how much to administer as well as how often. Doc Warner said the end was near, and that the sedative was likely the only thing that would keep her comfortable. It was hard to tell if she would last hours, days, or even a week. As she watched over her aunt, she prayed for a peaceful passing. She was certain that Gott knew best, and she continued to rely heavily upon her faith to get her through these long days and nights. She prayed daily for David too, fervently begging the Lord to spare him, so that they could continue to have a life together. Even if she had to care for a disabled husband, she would always be devoted to the man she loved.

A few agonizing days later, her aunt's breathing became extremely labored. The doctor was again summoned to the cottage. This time, there was no hope left for Eliza, as the doctor explained how much time was likely left,

"Die sunn is am unnergeh (*the sun is setting*) upon our schwester, Eliza, and we pray Gott to take her into his heavenly kingdom." Then Doc Warner sat in the kitchen along with the undertaker, awaiting the inevitable moment that Eliza's spirit would leave her earthly body. It happened late in the night, and Rachael allowed the men to do what was necessary to prepare Eliza for burial. A sad pall fell upon her as she thought about her aunt's last few months. She hoped against hope that David was not in similar circumstances. At least after the funeral, which the entire community attended, she would make the return trip to Pennsylvania. Brant readied the buggy once more, and off they went so that Rachael could nurse yet another ailing loved one. She was absolutely desperate to reach David's bedside. He needed her, and she needed him, and she continued her unwavering prayers to Gott. This time she felt little discomfort from the bumpy ride in the decrepit buggy, as her thoughts were entirely on David. It had been at least two weeks since she had heard word from the family. This was mostly due to the time it took to travel from Indiana to home, with several stops along the way to stay the nights. She refused to take proper care of herself, until Brant sat her down for a good talking to,

"Rachael, what good will this do for David? You must eat, sleep, and take proper care of yourself. He will need you to be fit as a fiddle, so that you can nurse him back to health!" Although he was completely uncertain whether there was much hope for David or not, he figured the best thing to do was to try to raise the girl's spirits. The last thing anyone needed was another sick person. Rachael was so worn out from caring for Eliza, that Brant was worried that David's condition would do her in for certain if things did not begin to change.

Late in the morning the next day, Brant drove the buggy towards her mamm's house. He helped her down by offering his hand as support, but she seemed weak and brokenhearted. Her mamm ran to greet them, and when Rachael spied her mother, she collapsed in exhaustion into her arms. Brant carried her into her bedroom, as her mamm prepared a meal for them both. He had driven through the night so that Rachael could arrive home as soon as possible. He felt horrified that she had not fared as well as he had hoped. Sometimes a broken heart was just as damaging if not more so than a broken bone. He had learned that when his own mamm had passed away nearly twenty years ago. She had been the backbone of his family, and he had been very close to her. He had to work hard to get back on track, because his family needed him to be strong. He sat with her parents for the next few nights, until she recovered properly. Her mamm's careful attention and loving care proved to be the most healing element besides the power of prayer. When everyone was sure that Rachael was much improved in both body and spirit, he bid the family farewell, and headed back to his village. Meanwhile, her mamm and daed debated over when to get her over to David's side. His condition had not changed since the beginning, and his parents were beginning to lose hope. It was difficult enough to lose a family member, but when it was a child it was a million times more painful. They came to the decision that Gloria would come to fetch her in the morning, and her mamm would pack another traveling bag for her daughter. Now that she was stronger, well-nourished, and back home, Rachael did her best to use all of her strength and faith to help David. She planned to stay by his side no matter the outcome. There was even talk of a symbolic ceremony to wed the two lovers, if the doctor decided there was little chance for regaining consciousness. No one uttered a word of these melancholy plans to Rachael, so everyone in the village continued to offer food and other home comforts that David's family needed. After the accident, his daed stopped the harvest, and it was up to his bruders and family friends to finish the essential work. It was the only way that the Todd's brought in any income, and Mr. Todd was forlorn with grief. He and his wife had the preacher visit every other day, and everyone gathered for a prayer circle. Rachael had brought back with her the finished wedding quilt. As soon as she saw him, she removed the drab blankets, wiped his brow, and wrapped him gently in the quilt. Hopefully, on some level, he could feel her presence and know that she was pouring all her love into caring for his every need. This also gave his parents a much-needed break to rest. They were thankful that she was now safely back home where she was dearly needed.

As she tended to her comatose lover, Rachael did her best to make his surroundings as cheerful as possible. She went out to the meadow, the place where he had proposed, and picked a bunch of wild flowers. She put several vases of sweet smelling buds around his pillows, so that he might sense the pretty aroma of that romantic day. She also spoke to him about the future, and read to him from the bible. She chose passages that spoke of love and how merciful Gott could be to those who clung to their faith. She prayed that these things combined would aid in helping David regain consciousness. She began to hum church hymns close to his ear while holding his hand. She recited possible names for their future children, and invented stories of family outings and special holiday gatherings. She told stories of them becoming grandparents in their later years, with all their grandchildren surrounding them. The Todd's even set up a special cot for her, so that he would always have her next to him. That way, just in case he came to, his intended would be there to greet him.

It was after all these tireless gestures, and long days and nights, that Rachael fell into a deep slumber. She had been singing to David, when she eventually drifted off to sleep with her head resting gently upon his chest. Her arms were folded around his neck in the careful cradle she often used when she sang close to his ear. This is how she fell asleep that night. And, in the morning, quite early just before sunrise, this was the way she awoke to soft whispers coming from David. His eyes were struggling to flutter open, and his hand quivered slightly within her own. She sat up immediately, still grasping his hand, and called out for the Todd's. The entire family gathered in the hallway outside his sickroom. His mamm and daed came into the room to see what the commotion was. David had finally woken up after so long! Rachael fell to his bedside,

"Oh, David! My love! You have returned to us..." and she wept tears of joy. She allowed his parents to have some private time with their son, while she ran to the kitchen with Gloria. They got busy preparing a very simple and plain breakfast of the nourishing foods that the doctor had written down if he came out of the coma. He would be extremely weak in the months to follow, and would have to adhere to strict bedrest for the ribs and legs to mend completely. Rachael made up a tray, complete with a few flowers from the meadow, and quickly shooed everyone away, so that he could eat his breakfast in peace and quiet. He still had quite a long road of recovery before him, and comfort and love were of the utmost importance in keeping his spirits up. He finished his meal the best he could, and gazed at Rachael. He blinked away a few tears, but was not yet able to speak. As David spent the next two months recovering, Rachael was always there to help him. She continued everything that she had been doing while he was in the coma, but added a few soft conversations as his speech was restored to him. She urged him to exercise his limbs that were movable to prevent bedsores and atrophy of his muscles. She helped his mamm and Gloria when he needed bathing, and they allowed her free reign of the kitchen to prepare all his meals. The two ate together in his room until he was strong enough to be wheeled out to the common table. A few farmers had taken up a collection to craft a wheelchair for David, so that he could get around before he was ready for crutches. That way, Rachael could sit with him on the front porch. They breathed in the fresh air, and David's health continued to improve,

"Rachael, tell me again how you came to me? How far did you travel to be at my side?"

"Darling, I was with my Aunt Eliza for some months, and got word from your mother about the accident. Do you remember falling from the ladder in the barn?" she asked.

"No, my memory is so foggy. All I can remember is floating across the sky over the beautiful meadow. I kept looking down to see how I was flying with no wings, and below I saw the two of us just like on that day. I would try to speak to them, to us, but the words would not come out. Then I recall an angelic voice singing songs from church, and it was almost as if it was someone calling me back to reality," recalled David, "it must have been your sweet singing that I was hearing in the distance. It was beckoning me homeward, but I was flying in the opposite direction towards a light."

"It sounds like you hovered between life and death. You were very unstable, and your heart rate was very slow at times. Perhaps all our prayers called you back to where you belong. Gott decided your time here was not yet finished. With my Aunt Eliza, despite our prayers, it was her time to go. Gott knows best when it is our time. But for you, Gott must have given you a purpose here with the people who love you! I always prayed for you, and when I did, I asked Him to spare you, so that we might have a life together. But we must be grateful for the blessings He has given to us. We must give back something special to our community, David. We must show our gratitude for the many gifts Gott has bestowed upon us."

"I agree wholeheartedly, my dear Rachael," continued David, and he seemed to hesitate to say anything more. He appeared sleepy, and it had been a long day. She wheeled him back inside, set out dinner for his family, and got him into bed,

"You need to be careful not to tax yourself too soon, David. Our marriage can wait until you are fully yourself again. I don't care how long it takes. Now lie down, and have pleasant dreams," and she kissed his forehead goodnight. She tucked the marriage quilt snugly around him, and David drifted off to sleep.

Yet another month passed by, and David was steadily gaining strength. His legs had healed, and he got back to walking slowly with a renewed sense of purpose. There was something very important that he had to do without Rachael's knowledge. One morning when Rachael was back at her own home visiting her family, David requested that his daed drive him to the preacher's house in town. He shared his secret with his father, because he knew how happy it would make his parents,

"Daed, I want the preacher to visit this afternoon and perform the wedding ceremony. I want to surprise Rachael. We only need our closest family members there, and a normal family meal. That is what truly matters to me, and I think then Rachael and I will move into the vacant cottage across from the preacher. I have a plan that I would like to run by the preacher, and if he agrees, then it would be best for Rachael and me to be near the center of town."

"What is the plan, David?" his father asked excitedly. But, David being David, he would not give away the idea he had been formulating for some time now.

"All in good time, Daed," and he smiled as they knocked upon the preacher's door. Pastor Robert answered, and invited the two men in to the sitting room. His wife prepared tea, and they sat down to discuss the viability of the ceremony to take place that afternoon, and then David requested to speak to Pastor Robert alone. They spoke only for about thirty minutes, and they rejoined Mr. Todd. Everyone piled into the buggy, and headed towards the Todd Farm. Once there, David shared his secret plans for the ceremony with his mamm and schwesters and bruders. Gloria and his other sister, May, made up some simple decorations of flower garlands, and draped them beautifully across the barn. The barn where the terrible accident had taken place had been completely renovated by the town's menfolk. It was part of the Amish tradition to raise new structures as a group. They had down a spectacular job, and the barn was still pristine. No animals had yet been relocated to the new barn. David had arranged for Rachael's mamm to bring her special wedding dress when they returned for the family meal that was planned since last week. Only her mamm was privy to David's plans for the romantic secret wedding in the barn.

As the morning waned, Rachael and her family prepared the buggies to drive her entire family over to the Todd's home. This was to be the very first gathering of the two families since their engagement announcement. Rachael was feeling a bit weary from waking so early, but was far too happy to succumb to sleepiness. As the buggies approached the Todd's farm, the Todd family was already outdoors, setting the long table for supper. Rachael and her mamm went towards the house to help Mrs. Todd and Gloria with the meal, and the men and boys toured the farm, and played ball. Just as Rachael thought it was time to summon everyone back to the outdoor table, her mamm took her aside, and presented her with the dress,

"Mamm! Why did you bring this? David and I have not set a date yet! Did you bring it to show Mrs. Todd?"

"No, dear daughter. Today is the day you must wear the gown. It is your wedding day," she cried, and Rachael stood aghast at the surprising news,

"How did you know? Did David plan this whole thing?" she exclaimed.

"Yes, of course he did. What else would you expect from him? He loves you more than words can describe, as I'm certain you know! Hurry on up, and put that dress on," she ordered,

"no more time to stand about with your mouth open." And mother and daughter laughed as they dressed Rachael for one of the most important days of her life.

Dusk had fallen, and the men had been busy hanging lanterns all around the barn area. The barn itself was lit with only candlelight and the flower garlands. It was a picture of pure beauty, yet simple as can be. Rachael's daed escorted her towards the barn. Once inside, she marveled at how ethereal it all appeared, and then she looked at David who stood proudly ready to make her his wife. The preacher performed the ceremony, and they all headed towards the long and fully laden table under the lanterns and stars. Everyone took their seats, and a hush fell upon the table as David remained standing,

"Today has been the happiest day of my life. Rachael cared for me like an angel, and now we are married! But before we sit down to this delicious looking meal, I have something very important to announce, both to our family members, and to my dear wife."

Rachael came to stand beside him, for this was something she and David had already privately discussed, but she had not known that tonight was the night to announce his big project. Her heart was overflowing with pride and love for the man that she nearly lost to a tragic accident. Gott had spared him, and allowed them this special life. She was extremely excited to start this chapter of their lives together, especially since David was ready to announce their plans,

"Today, family, and Pastor Robert, we stand together in joy instead of sadness. It is important to note that Rachael was almost made a widow before she even had the chance to be a married woman. Too many women in our community have lost husbands to early deaths or tragic accidents. Rachael and I are beginning a charity that will serve the women that have suffered such a devastating loss. We will be living in town near Pastor Robert, and we shall be coordinating our efforts with neighboring communities, including our Englischer neighbors. The services we will provide will be open to any who are in need whether Amish or not. It is our way of thanking Gott for his blessings, and allowing us this very special day!"

There was clapping and cheering from around the table, as Pastor Robert recited the grace. It was certainly a night no one would ever forget, and it was the beginning of the beautiful promise that David had made to his beloved Rachael so long ago in the meadow.

# KAYLA

MONICA MARKS

It was Kayla's favorite time of year and when she woke that morning, she inhaled deeply, absorbing the nostalgic feeling which the onset of autumn brought along.

*It is time for harvest and engagement announcements,* she thought happily, swinging her long legs off the single mattress and scurrying to the window to stare into to endless farmland. The smallest frost had settled overnight but there was no cause for concern; the sunshine was fighting to warm the October day already and it was just past dawn. She tried to ignore the near exhaustion in her bones and stretched, willing herself to wake up.

*I slept more than enough,* she reasoned with her weary body. *There is no reason for me to be so tired.*

She told herself that the crisp fall air would invigorate her.

"Kayla!"

Her younger sister, Hannah threw open the door to her bedroom and folded her small arms across her chest.

"Haven't you dressed yet? It is almost seven o'clock!"

"Haven't you learned to knock yet? You are almost eight years old," Kayla replied haughtily. The sisters stared at each other before bursting into laughter.

"I am coming, Hannah," she assured the child. "There is time for breakfast and to walk to school."

Hannah smiled and Kayla clapped her hands.

"You lost another tooth!" she declared, rushing forward to examine her sister's mouth. "Let me see."

Hannah opened her mouth obligingly and the older sister patted her cheek.

"Go show *Daed* now," she instructed. "I will be along in a moment."

Hannah turned to leave Kayla, rushing down the steps toward the kitchen and Kayla hurried to change.

Hannah was not wrong; she had slept in again. It seemed to be happening with more frequency and Kayla had first believed the change of weather had been affecting her but suddenly she was not so certain.

*I must eat better,* she chided herself, slipping into a dark brown work dress and fastening an apron atop her skirt. *Autumn is not the time to waste time sleeping when Daed needs help with harvest and winter preparations. If you are so tired when the days are still long, what will you be like in two months?*

She padded across the threshold and into the corridor, trying to recall what needed to be done that morning. Canning needed to be started, the hay baled, pickling, jams...the list was endless as always and Kayla began to form a list in her mind in order of importance.

Slipping down the stairs, Kayla was suddenly overwhelmed by a wave of dizziness. She clutched the bannister, blood draining from her face as she tried to gather her bearings.

*Oh Gotte, I do not have the luxury of being sick,* she warned herself, willing a feeling of normalcy to come but in seconds, her legs had buckled and to her horror, Kayla tumbled down the remaining three steps onto the landing.

*Not again!* She thought, horrified, knowing that her family would witness her embarrassment this time. It was the third fainting spell she had experienced in two weeks but gratefully, her father and sister had not seen the others.

As spots of black and red danced before her eyes, she opened her mouth to moan but she began to lose consciousness as Hannah came running into the foyer, their father in tow.

The last thing she recalled before the world went dark was her small sister screaming.

When she woke, Jeremiah Roth stood praying over her, his eyes closed but even without reading the expression in his gentle blue irises, Kayla could see the concern in his face.

"*Daed*?" she called weakly, struggling to sit up against the bed. She realized she had been put back in her room, tucked in snugly among blankets.

"Oh, Kayla!" Jeremiah gasped, his lids flying open at the sound of her voice. "You must remain still. I have asked the Fishers to call for Dr. Imhoff."

"I am fine, *Daed*," Kayla protested. "It was nothing, I am sure. It happens sometimes."

"How many times?" Jeremiah demanded, his cornflower blue eyes wide with shock. "Why did you not tell me before?"

"It is no cause for alarm. Cancel the doctor!" Kayla groaned.

"Hush, *liebchen*," he insisted, pointing at the bed. "You will remain here until the doctor has seen you."

"We haven't time for this," Kayla insisted, attempting to rise again. "We have much to do."

"I am your father," Jeremiah growled with uncharacteristic sternness. "You will do as you are told. The harvest can wait."

Kayla settled back, blinking.

"All right, *Daed*," she relented. "I will wait but the Dr. Imhoff will tell you there is nothing wrong."

"I would rather hear it from him," Jeremiah replied. "He is the one with the medical degree after all."

He turned to the bedside and produced a glass of water.

"Drink this. I will wait downstairs Jonah."

"Where is Hannah?"

"Lydia Fisher has taken her to school. You mustn't worry, Kayla. All is tended to this morning. Your job is to rest."

He turned to leave the room before Kayla could form another argument, leaving her to stare at the ceiling is mild exasperation.

*This is foolish,* she thought but she dared not express her feelings aloud. She knew her father was concerned and she had no one to blame but herself.

*I have been neglecting meals and sleeping poorly,* she chided herself. *Now I have worried everyone.*

In minutes, she heard footfalls on the stairs and the door opened.

"*Guter mayire*, Kayla," Dr. Imhoff announced, smiling in his kindly way. "I understand you had a small fainting episode this morning."

Kayla stifled a sigh.

"It was nothing," she insisted.

"I will see about that," Jonah Imhoff replied lightly, opening his bag.

He checked her eyes and throat, running her temperature and pinching her skin to test for validity.

Then he turned to Jeremiah.

"We will talk outside," he told the patriarch, patting Kayla's face warmly.

"You should rest today, Kayla," he told her, closing his bag. Kayla chewed on her tongue to keep a thousand objections from erupting and watched helplessly as the men retreated into the hallway.

She strained her ears to listen, catching only a few words as she did.

"...tests...color...must be vigilant."

Their voices cut in and out but Kayla felt a prickle slide down her back as she understood the gist of their conversation.

*He believes there is something wrong with me,* she realized, concern floating through her for the first time since the incidents had begun. She tried to dismiss the feeling of worry but when her father returned to the bedroom, his eyes shone with something she had not seen in many years.

"Jonah is arranging for you to have tests done at Lancaster General Hospital," he told her gravely. Kayla swallowed quickly, realizing there was a lump in her throat.

"What does he believe is wrong, *Daed*?" she whispered and Jeremiah seemed to recognize his mistake, wiping the dismayed frown from his face.

"Nothing specific, *liebchen,*" he replied quickly. "It is merely a precaution. Do not fret; we will learn what ails you soon enough."

"*Daed,* I am certain it is - "

"You are not a doctor, Kayla. In the meanwhile, you will rest. I will see if Lydia can stay with you while I tend to the farm," he continued and Kayla heard no room for debate in his tone.

"*Daed,* you cannot tend the farm alone," she sighed. "You would better have Lydia help you."

Jeremiah stared at her for a long while as if he was looking directly through her.

"You are correct," he told her softly. "I must enlist help until you are better."

Without another word, he spun and walked from the bedroom, leaving Kayla to stare after him with her mouth agape in question.

The wagon drew near the farmhouse, Lydia Fisher leading the horse through the grey day. They were returning from Kayla's appointment at the hospital where she had undergone bloodwork for her ever increasing fainting and general fatigue.

"Would you like me to come with you, Kayla?" Lydia asked as she slid from the bench onto the dirt. Kayla stifled a sigh and shook her head, forcing a smile onto her lips. She was growing tired of being coddled by both her father and the neighbors, despite their good intentions.

"I feel fine," she fibbed. In reality, she wished to lay down but she dared not say anything to Lydia. The last thing she wished to do was cause more of a fuss.

"I will be by later this evening to fix supper for you," Lydia told her, picking up the reins. "Back to bed now."

Kayla did not answer but waved at the butcher's wife as she made her way from the Roth farm toward her own.

*I will go mad if I have to spend one more minute in bed,* Kayla thought glumly, turning toward the fields. She saw her father in the distance, reaping corn and she longed to run toward him but she did not. She would only interrupt him and take more time from his duties.

*Duties I should be tending to also,* she told herself, guilt wracking her body.

The doctor at the hospital had been candid with her assessment, citing several reasons for her strange illness.

"But we will run the necessary tests, Kayla and determine the cause."

It was not until Kayla and Lydia were almost home that she realized that the physician had told her nothing of sustenance.

*I can only wait for the results – however long that will take. In the meanwhile, Daed is working alone on the farm.*

Suddenly, another figure appeared, close to the entrance of the maize and Kayla started.

"Hello!" she called out, her brow furrowing with concern. The stranger turned to look at her and he seemed to freeze as they stared at one another.

"Hello," he replied, turning to face her. Kayla stepped back in surprise as he emerged from the stalks, dressed in pair of blue jeans and a black and red flannel shirt.

"Who are you?" she demanded as she stared at him uncomprehendingly. "Does my father know you are here?"

The dark-haired man paused, cocking his head to the side slightly, a single strand of hair falling directly onto his forehead.

"Yes," he answered. "My name is Will. Will Jenkins."

Kayla waited for him to elaborate on why he stood on their land but he did not speak. Slowly, she drew closer to him.

"Why are you on our land?" Kayla asked, her green eyes narrowing in suspicion. She loathed that she was immediately concerned about the Englisher's presence but she could not reconcile one good reason that the man would be on the property.

"I am helping with the harvest," Will told her simply.

"Helping whom?"

Will stared at her for a long moment as if he was concerned she was slow-witted.

"I am helping the owner of the land obviously," he replied dryly. "Who are you?"

Kayla was reluctant to disclose any information to the man, her eyes lifting to see where her father was in the field.

*Daed wouldn't hire an Englisher to help on the farm,* she thought, distrustful of Will Jenkins. *And he certainly did not mention bringing on any help.*

To her relief, she was Jeremiah approaching.

"There is my father now," Kayla said sternly. "If you do not belong here, you best run along before he catches you on our property."

Will gave her a bemused smile.

"If I ran along, I would not be doing my job," he told her lightly. "I think your father would be angrier at that."

"Kayla you are home," Jeremiah cried, hurrying toward his daughter. She watched as he glanced nervously at the stranger.

"Come inside and we will talk," the senior Roth said, without acknowledging the Englisher in their midst. Kayla opened her mouth to speak but the look in her father's eye silenced her.

"Yes, *Daed,*" she agreed, turning to follow Jeremiah inside the house. Will remained in place, his mouth upturned and Kayla cast him one long look before entering the house.

"Daed, did you hire that Englisher to help with the harvest?" she asked dubiously.

"Yes, but that is unimportant. Tell me what the doctor said," Jeremiah told her, abruptly changing the conversation.

"But *Daed*, I will be fine soon. You did not need to hire anyone, especially not an outsider!" Kayla cried.

Jeremiah's mouth became a fine line and his eyes narrowed.

"I do not wish to discuss the Englisher," he told her flatly. "I asked you about the doctor. What was said and what tests were done?"

Kayla swallowed another question.

"She believes that it is a blood disorder of sorts but I will not know until the tests come back. Simple bloodwork was performed. I will return next week for the results."

Jeremiah's brow knitted and he nodded.

"What sort of blood disorder?"

Kayla shrugged.

"I do not know, Daed. She did not give me specifics. I can only wait to learn."

Jeremiah did not seem happy with her answer but Kayla had little else to give him.

"Go rest now, Kayla. I will come to you after the work is done."

"*Daed*, may I go for Hannah? I do not wish to spend one more minute in bed. Please?"

Jeremiah regarded her for a long moment before bobbing his head reluctantly.

"If you are certain you are not feeling ill, you may pick up your sister from school. But you must come straight back to bed. Understood?"

Gratefully, Kayla nodded and hurried toward the front door before he could change his mind.

*It will be lovely to stretch my legs and inhale the fresh autumn air*, she thought. She was beginning to feel as a caged rabbit.

As she walked toward the road, she found herself looking back at Will Jenkins. He was hard at work, paying her no mind but as she turned in the direction of the schoolhouse, Kayla thought she could feel eyes on her.

*Who is this man and what is he doing here?*

That evening, Lydia Fisher came as promised, preparing a delicious supper for the Roths before heading home to her own family.

"She is a blessing to us," Jeremiah commented when she left and they sat down to eat. Kayla scowled slightly.

"She really doesn't need be here quite so often, *Daed*," she told her father. "I can still work."

"Your health is paramount, Kayla. Lydia has four able sons to work their farm and can spare a hand until you are well."

"I am well!" Kayla grunted, trying to keep the frustration from her voice. Jeremiah shot her a warning look and Kayla clamped her mouth closed. Arguing would not prove fruitful.

"Tell me about the Englisher," Kayla said instead and Hannah's head jerked upward from her stew.

"What Englisher?" the little girl asked curiously. Jeremiah's scowl deepened and he shook his head almost imperceivably at his oldest daughter.

"I have already explained that Will is helping with the harvest. There is nothing else to tell."

"Where did you find him, *Daed*? You must admit that it is odd to bring an outsider here when there are many in the community whom you could call upon for help."

Jeremiah's blue eyes seemed to darken.

"I am the head of this house," he snapped. "I do not need to answer to you for my choices."

Kayla was stung by his tone and she bit her lower lip. It was unlike her father to speak crossly to her or Hannah.

*Whatever silliness is happening with me is causing him stress,* she determined, taking a spoonful of beef stew. *I must not give him more of a reason to worry.*

She did not mention Will again but she decided that she would speak to Will the next time she saw him and learn more about him.

Kayla had her chance the following day. Jeremiah went to sell their goods at market, leaving Kayla alone.

"I have asked Lydia to come later in the day to ensure you are well," her father told her. Kayla rolled her eyes where he could not see.

*You must not get annoyed,* she warned herself but she could not help but feel frustrated at being treated like a child. She knew that was not Jeremiah's intention but she could not release the slight resentment she was feeling.

Her mother had died when she was fourteen, leaving Kayla as the woman of the household. Hannah was still an infant and Kayla had learned to tend to both the baby and the farm.

Standing idle was not something which she did well and she wished desperately that the doctors would quickly diagnose her issue so she was able to resume her role in the family and on the farm.

"Thank you, *Daed*," she said instead of unleashing the barrage of protests vying to spring from her lips.

"I do not want you to leave the house today, Kayla," Jeremiah told her seriously as he stood in the doorway of her bedroom. "Stay inside and preferably in bed. If you are to faint with no one nearby..."

"I will not faint!" she cried but Jeremiah shook his head.

"You have no way of assuring me of that," he replied. "Please heed my words, Kayla. I speak only out of concern for you."

Begrudgingly, Kayla nodded.

"Yes, *Daed,*" she agreed. "I will take Hannah to school and – "

"No," Jeremiah said sharply. "Lydia will take your sister to school."

Kayla gritted her teeth and nodded.

"Have a good day in town, *Daed*," Kayla sighed. She watched as he retreated to the freshly loaded wagon and disappeared down the road.

*I have become a prisoner in my own home,* Kayla thought mournfully, folding her arms across her chest. She wondered what she would do for the remainder of the day and as she thought it, she watched a silver sedan car driving up the road which Jeremiah had just taken.

Kayla leaned forward, watching the dilapidated vehicle pull onto their land, her pulse quickening. As she peered at the driver, she realized it was Will Jenkins arriving to work.

*Is he supposed to be here today?* She wondered nervously. If so, why hadn't her father told her to expect him.

Will jumped from the driver's seat and she noted he was wearing the same clothes he had the day before. He did not seem to notice her observing him, pulling a few items which she could not see from the backseat before turning toward the barn.

As Kayla rose her hand to wave in greeting, something tugged on her skirt.

"Kayla, I am hungry!" Hannah announced from behind her, causing the older girl to jump.

"You startled me, Hannah!" she chided and Hannah shrugged indifferently. She turned to usher her sister into the house, eyeing Will who had vanished behind the house.

*I wonder if I should tend to him,* she thought but her father's words reverberated in her mind.

*"I do not want you to leave the house today, Kayla. Stay inside and preferably in bed. If you are to faint with no one nearby..."*

She pushed the thought of Will Jenkins from her mind and closed the door.

She had no reason to approach the Englisher.

The weather had turned unseasonably warm and Kayla lifted her head from her book, realizing that the front room had grown almost stifling hot.

She cast the novel aside and reached to open the window, gazing into the fields. To her surprise, she saw Will Jenkins standing near the maple tree beside his car, wiping sweat from his brow.

Kayla watched him for a moment and she could see the sun and hard work had turned his face red.

*He must be thirsty. He is dressed much too warmly to work the fields in that attire,* she realized, rising from window seat.

A cool glass of water in hand, Kayla stepped into the yard. Will's back was to her and she tried to make herself heard as to not surprise him.

He turned and Kayla was filled with a strange sense of familiarity suddenly, something she had not felt the previous afternoon.

"Hello," he said and Kayla nodded, handing him the glass of water.

"It is very hot today," she volunteered. "I thought you might be thirsty."

He nodded gratefully and accepted the beverage, drinking it in one long gulp.

"I will fetch you another one," she offered and he shook his head.

"No, thank you," he replied. "I should be getting back to work."

He was older than Kayla with dark hair and vivid green eyes. His face seemed it had not been shaved in four days and there were dark circles under his eyes.

*He is handsome in a rugged sort of way,* she thought, studying his face. The feeling that she knew him did not diminish.

"As you wish," she replied, turning back.

"Actually wait," Will called nervously. He peered at his gloved hands in embarrassment as Kayla turned back to him.

"Yes?"

"Maybe one more glass of water," he muttered and Kayla smiled.

"Of course."

Inside the house, she thought of the somewhat bedraggled man on her lawn and she again wondered where he had come from.

*If he has no water, he likely has no food either,* she realized and quickly went to work preparing him a snack. *If he doesn't eat, he will also faint. Daed doesn't need to come home to such a sight.*

She did not want to think what her father would say if he knew she was feeding the Englisher.

Outside, she gestured for him to sit and eat. The gratitude in his face was beyond anything she had ever seen and a mixture of sadness and pity overwhelmed her.

"Are you from Lancaster, Mr. Jenkins?" Kayla asked timidly as he inhaled the bread and cheese she had brought to him. He shook his head and she waited for him to swallow the morsels before answering.

"No," he replied. "I am from Reading."

Kayla's brow furrowed.

"Reading?" she asked in surprise. "You have a little bit of a journey to make here."

Will nodded and shrugged his shoulders.

"It is an hour's drive," he answered. "But your father offered me very good pay and gas money for the trip."

None of what he said made sense to Kayla.

*Why would Daed bring an Englisher to the district from an hour away?*

"You know, I don't even know your name," Will commented as he polished off the last of the light meal she provided for him.

Embarrassed, Kayla extended her hand.

"Kayla Roth."

Will accepted her outstretched palm and they two looked at one another for a long moment. Kayla felt a sudden confusion as she stared at him.

*Why do I feel such an affinity with this man?* She wondered, an almost awe-struck feeling overcoming her.

"Nice to meet you, Kayla. I should be getting back to work. I don't want your dad to think he's wasting his money."

Kayla stepped back reluctantly, wanting to speak with him longer but she knew he was right. There was much work to be done and she had detained the harvest enough already.

"If you should need more water, Mr. Jenkins," Kayla told him. "There is a spigot beside the barn."

He looked at her thankfully.

"You truly are a lifesaver, Miss Roth. You and your father have helped me a great deal already."

Kayla did not know how to respond but Will did not seem to require an answer.

She slipped back into the house and reclaimed her window seat but her book was forgotten. She spent the remainder of the afternoon watching Will working in the field and wondering if *Gotte* had sent him to their farm for a reason.

Kayla waited impatiently for her father to take Hannah to school before hurrying outside to greet Will who was cleaning the stalls. Her father would not be gone long but she wanted to talk to the man again, if only for a short time.

"Good morning, Miss Roth," Will said brightly. She smiled.

"You may call me Kayla," she told him. "I brought you muffins if you are hungry."

She offered them to him and he took them happily. For the third day, he donned the same clothes and Kayla wondered if he had any other garments.

*He is obviously not well off. I wonder if that is why Daed brought him here; to help a man down on his luck.*

"In that case, you can call me Will," he laughed, taking a bite of the muffin in his hand. His dark eyebrows shot up.

"This is great!" he said. "Did you make this yourself?"

She nodded.

"The Amish can do everything," he sighed. "I knew an Amish girl once. She never failed to amaze me with her talents."

"What happened to her?" Kayla asked curiously, leaning against a stall door. Will smiled thinly.

"She returned to her community. Decided the outside world wasn't for her after all."

Kayla could read the regret in his face but before she could ask anything else, she felt herself grow lightheaded.

*Oh no!* She thought as bright lights colored her line of sight.

"Kayla?" Will's voice sounded very far away and suddenly she was in his arms as her legs buckled beneath her. She willed herself to take deep breaths and to her relief she did not faint.

"Are you all right?" Will demanded as she regained her footing. Slowly he released her and Kayla stood on shaking legs.

She nodded, shifting her eyes downward.

"I get fainting spells sometimes," she confessed as the spots cleared from her vision. Will's emerald eyes narrowed.

"Have you been to the doctor?" he asked and Kayla bobbed her head.

"I am awaiting test results," she told him, sighing. "They believe it is some sort of blood disorder."

Will's mouth became a tight, white line.

"Is that so?" he asked quietly.

"Kayla! What are you doing in here?" Jeremiah appeared in the doorway, his face pale as he took in the scene before him.

"I – I came to offer Mr. Jenkins some muffins," she murmured, averting her eyes from his shocked face.

"You should not be in here," he told his daughter, shooing her from the barn.

"Thank you for the muffins, Kayla," Will called after her. "I hope you are feeling better."

Jeremiah led the way back to the house and did not say a word until they were inside, whirling to confront Kayla.

"Why were you speaking with Will Jenkins?" he demanded furiously. "I told you that you are to stay in the house."

"Daed, I am growing mad staying in the house!" Kayla protested. "And Will seems a very nice man!"

Jeremiah's expression was indecipherable as he stared at his oldest daughter. He seemed to be considering his next words carefully.

"You are to stay away from Will Jenkins," he told her firmly. "I do not want you anywhere near him, do you understand?"

Kayla's eyebrows knit together.

"No," she answered truthfully. "Of course I do not understand. Why would you ask me to stay away from him?"

"He is not someone whom you should associate yourself," Jeremiah insisted. Kayla stared at him uncomprehendingly.

"*Daed*, if he is such a terrible man, why would you have him come to our home?"

"He not in our home. He is merely helping with harvest. I want you to swear that you will not have any further contact with him. Swear it, Kayla!"

Kayla did not know what to say. She wanted to promise her father that she wouldn't see the Englisher again but she knew her curiosity would not keep her away.

"Kayla!"

She hung her head and nodded, sighing deeply.

"I swear it, *Daed*," she breathed but she wondered if she would be able to honor her oath.

Kayla did not risk going to Will until the next time her father went to the market, three days later. She found herself watching the worker from the window often, willing him to take notice of her and sometimes he would lift his head and acknowledge her with a half-wave but never in Jeremiah's presence.

*This makes little sense. Daed brings him from out of town to work and then speaks as if the man is a danger to us.*

The previous day, she had gone to the hospital for her test results.

"As we suspected, Kayla, you have a blood disorder called megaloblastic anemia. It can be treated with supplements and dietary changes but it is manageable," the doctor informed her. Kayla nodded, relieved the diagnosis was simple.

"When will I be able to resume my work?" she asked eagerly and the doctor chuckled.

"We will start your injections immediately and you should notice a change within a week or so. The fatigue and dizziness will lessen and you will be back to normal in no time."

Kayla peered at the physician.

"What causes this?" she asked with interest.

"In your case, it is genetic," the doctor replied.

After Hannah left for school and her father for the market, Kayla rushed outside to speak with Will.

"Kayla, you should not be out here," he told her, his jaw locking when she appeared. Kayla was hurt by his words.

"I do not understand; why does my father wish to keep me away from you?" she asked bluntly but Will did not answer as he continued to bale hay.

"I'm sorry," she muttered, turning away. "I only came to tell you that I got my results from the hospital. I have a blood disorder – anemia."

Will's head jerked up to stare at her, his mouth open slightly.

"What kind of anemia?" he demanded. Kayla wracked her mind to recall the proper term.

"Mega...mega..."

"Megaloblastic?"

Kayla smiled.

"Yes, that is it."

Kayla waited for him to return her grin but his face went dark.

"You should go back in the house. You don't want your father to catch you out here."

She stared at him, tears of humiliation filling her eyes.

*I thought we had a bond,* she thought miserably, chewing on her lower lip.

"Hurry up," Will growled, pointing at the house. Kayla spun, tears spilling down her cheeks as she ran back inside.

*Daed was right; I should have just stayed away from him.*

"Kayla! *Daed* is yelling!" Hannah cried, flying into the kitchen where Kayla was doing the dishes.

"What?"

"He is yelling at the Englisher!" Hannah insisted, pointing toward the front of the house. Kayla quickly dried her hands on her apron and rushed toward the door. As she pulled open the heavy wood, she heard a car door slam and watched as Will screeched away in his rundown sedan.

Jeremiah stood, his arms folded angrily across his chest as he watched the man leave and Kayla was sure she had never seen him look so intimidating.

"*Daed*! *Daed*, what happened?" she cried, rushing toward him. He whirled to face her, his face undergoing several expressions, settling on near-panic.

"Nothing," he replied gruffly. "Go inside."

"*Daed* please!" she begged. "What happened with Will?"

His eyes narrowed dangerously and he shook his head.

"I made a mistake bringing him here," he muttered, storming toward the house. "Do not mention his name in this house again."

Bewildered, Kayla turned toward the road but of course Will was long gone.

She looked helplessly at her father but she was only staring at his retreating back and Kayla was filled with an inexplicable sense of loss.

*He is not coming back,* she realized and the thought made her sick to her stomach for reasons she could not comprehend.

Life on the Roth farm returned to normal and as promised, Kayla began to feel better as the treatments took effect.

The harvest went well and Will Jenkins did not return to the district but his memory was fresh in Kayla's mind.

*Perhaps one day, Daed will tell me who he was truly and how he came to be here.* But she did not have high hopes for that occurring. Jeremiah never brought up the Englisher again and Kayla did not dare.

It was the beginning of November when the letter arrived.

It was slipped between the screen door and it had not been mailed.

Without opening it, Kayla suspected she knew who had written it but as she tore into the envelope, her suspicions were confirmed.

Her hands trembling, she read the letter, her heart thumping wildly.

*Dear Kayla,* it read. *I have wrestled with whether to write this letter or leave well enough alone as your father wanted. I can't live my life without telling you who I am because I think you deserve the truth. As you know, my name is William Jenkins. Twenty years ago, I met a beautiful girl in Lancaster and we fell madly in love. I mentioned that I once knew an Amish girl and that girl was your mother, Anna. We had plans to marry but one day, I woke up and she was gone. She had left me a letter, much like the one I am writing you, apologizing for her choice and claiming she had made a mistake leaving her community. She begged me not to look for her and I agreed. I left town and moved to Reading, not wanting to run into her. If I had stayed, I would have learned that she married Jeremiah Roth and soon gave birth to a beautiful baby daughter; you.*

*If I had not seen your eyes, I may never have known that you were mine but there is no mistaking you are my child.*

*I did not understand why your father had brought me to your farm until I heard you were sick. Megaloblastic anemia is genetic — I know because I have it also. I suspect Jeremiah was terribly concerned for your health and wanted to learn about your family history. I don't think he ever intended for us to meet and when we did and I learned the truth, he grew angry and banished me from the farm. I want you to know that if I had known you were my child, I would have always been in your life.*

*You may do what you wish with this information, Kayla. You may choose to never see me again or you may confront your father. Shamefully I do not know you well enough to know how you will react but I would like to get to know you. You are a grown woman and I can't force a relationship on you.*

*Whatever you do, please remember that your father only did what he did to keep you safe, happy and healthy. If you decide to let him know that you know, go easy on him. He is the only father you have ever had after all.*

*I have enclosed my phone number and mailing address. I will not hold my breath but I will hold onto hope that you will see me again.*

*Whatever you choose, know that I support you and love you. I wish you only the best this world has to offer.*

*Love always,*

*Will*

Tears flowed freely down Kayla's face and the words grew blurry as she read and re-read the letter, her breath escaping in shuddering sobs.

"Oh Gotte, Kayla!" Jeremiah cried, entering the foyer where his oldest daughter stood. "What happened?"

Kayla shook her head and stuffed the letter back into the envelope, wiping her face with the back of her hand.

"Nothing, nothing," she gasped. He stared at her, his face a mask of worry and Kayla had never been filled with so much love for another person.

*Does he know I know? Has he been filled with worry for the past nineteen years that the truth would come out and he would lose the daughter he had raised as his own?* Kayla could not imagine the pain her father must have endured over the years.

*He is the only father I have ever known. He is my Daed no matter what that letter reads.*

Impulsively, she threw herself into her father's arm, burying her face in his broad chest.

"I love you, *Daed*," she whispered, inhaling the comforting scent of his dirty work clothes.

"I love you, daughter," he sighed.

In that moment, Kayla knew she would honor her father's wishes and never again bring up Will Jenkin's name in their home.

That did not mean she would never see the Englisher again.

# A BROKEN AMISH HEART

## TERRI DOWNES

"Do you think it's the latch?" asked Sarah, looking up at the door.

The rattling sound had persisted all the way through church service, and even when two of the boys had moved a chair to lean against the door, the door had rattled and buzzed with every gust of wind.

"Maybe," said Sarah's best friend, Sadie, barely glancing at the door. "What were you saying?"

"I was asking if you'd noticed anything about my *daed*," said Sarah. "If you thought anything had... changed."

The door rattled again. Sarah reached out and pressed lightly against the latch, to feel whether or not it was responsible for the sound, but there was no change. She pressed harder.

"What are you doing?" asked Sadie.

"I have an idea... so did you notice anything?"

"I think you'd be more likely to notice than me," Sadie pointed out. "What sort of thing are you talking about?"

"Just sort of... the things he's saying, I guess."

Sarah looked back up at the door, and tried pressing against the hinges. Still nothing.

"I know you wouldn't notice so much as me, but he's been up at your place every spare moment these past two weeks. I've only seen him for the odd meal here or there. I thought maybe you might have picked up on something."

"Oh. Well, he's not been in the house," said Sadie. "He and my *daed* and the boys have been working on the cottage, and that's all the way down the end of the property."

"Right, of course."

The cottage on Sadie's family's farm had previously only ever been rented out to seasonal laborers, and had been kept in a rough, unfinished state. But it had recently been let to a newcomer to the community – a widow. Sadie's mother had insisted that the cottage be made suitable for a lady occupant.

The door was still rattling. Sarah tried its corners. Bottom left, top left, top right – *there* it was. As she pushed against the corner of the door, the rattling stopped. She let go, and it started again.

"I was just wondering if anything had happened," continued Sarah. She grabbed a piece of paper from the basket of kindling scraps by the door and started folding it up. "He's been talking about *mamme*."

"Really?" Sadie looked surprised.

"I know. The first time in years."

"Just..." Sadie hesitated delicately. "Just your *mamme*? Not..."

"Not Mary, no."

John rarely spoke of his dead wife – but he never, never spoke of Mary.

Sarah reached up and wedged the folded piece of paper into the gap between the corner of the door and its frame. The noise stopped.

"Good job," said Sadie, looking up at the door.

"Girls!" called Sadie's mother, Elsa, from inside the kitchen. "Come on, the first load of dishes need doing."

"Coming, *mamme*," called Sadie. She turned back to Sarah. "Tell you what. I'll keep an eye out for any time I see your *daed* this week."

"But they're done with the cottage, aren't they?" Now it was Sarah's turn to be surprised. "I thought – the widow, what's her name?"

"Miriam. Miriam – uh, Stolzfus."

"I thought she had moved in already."

"She has, three days ago," affirmed Sadie. "They were just going to finish whitewashing the outside, but I heard your *daed* tell mine that the roof needed work as well. He said he'd be coming over next week to see to it."

Sarah shook her head as they made their way into the kitchen. Why hadn't he said anything to her about this?

***

"That's her?"

Sadie nodded, helping herself to potatoes.

"She's beautiful."

The widow, standing and speaking to Sadie's mother and father across the yard, was truly lovely. She was tall, two inches taller than Sarah. Her skin looked clear and free of lines, her hair was smooth and dark, her features finely set.

Sarah was not sure why she was surprised. Perhaps it was because all the widows she had known in her life had been over the age of sixty.

As she watched, Sarah saw her father walk over to the little group.

It was odd, Sarah thought, the way he walked. She was used to him walking with his head downcast – just a little, not so as anyone would really notice. Not unless they were looking. Not unless they had known him as he had been before.

Maybe it was all that time he had spent with Sadie's father and her brothers recently, Sarah thought. For the past three years, John had kept to himself as much as possible, only joining in with group events when it was something that the entire community was expected at, like the occasional barn raising.

Sarah had been the one to suggest he go over and help set up the new cottage, lending his construction skills. She had thought it would be good for him to get out of the house, though she had almost not expected him to agree.

Socializing was clearly good for him. She watched him talking, now, and he looked happy. He almost never looked happy. He had obviously rekindled his friendship with Sadie's parents, and he was even talking to the widow, whom he must have met when she moved into the cottage.

Yes, thought Sarah. It was good that he would be returning the following week to continue to work on the cottage, even if it did mean that she would be spending more time alone.

Later, Sarah was given an opportunity to meet the widow herself.

She had kept busy, helping with the serving, and had not really spoken to anyone. Then, during the normal time of socializing afterward, she had continued to catch up with Sadie, whom she had not seen much of in the past few weeks as she had also been helping prepare the cottage.

"It seems like you've all been working non stop on that place," Sarah commented to Sadie as they stood together in the shade of an oak tree at the side of the yard.

They had finished helping to clean, and were now watching as the tables and chairs were packed back into their long wagon.

"We only had the two weeks," said Sadie. "That was when we got her Miriam's letter asking if she could rent the place."

"You mean she only took the place at two weeks notice? That seems odd."

Sadie shrugged. "She'd been living with her brother since her husband died. Then he decided to get married, and she wanted to give his new wife the run of the house without worrying about her."

"Hmm," said Sarah. "I wonder if that means she didn't get on with the brother's wife. Do you think?"

Perhaps the new wife was unpleasant, or controlling. Or maybe Miriam herself was not that easy to get on with...

"Who knows," said Sadie, distracted by the sight of her seven-year-old brother darting in amongst the men who were lifting the heavy wooden folding tables. He knocked against one of the men, who almost lost his grip on the end he was carrying.

"Andrew!" Sadie called out. "Careful!"

"*Mamme* said I could help," Andrew called back, attempting to grasp the side of a table that was being lifted.

"He's going to hurt himself," said Sadie worriedly, waving over at her mother.

Elsa, coming out if the kitchen, immediately sized up the situation and beckoned Andrew over to her.

"You said I could help," he began, sounding put out.

"Of course," said his mother. "But I have a more important job for you. Can you be very strong, and help me carry all of the dishwashing tubs down into the cellar?"

Andrew, puffing himself up with importance, hurried into the kitchen.

Sarah and Sadie laughed.

"I always preferred that method myself," came a voice to their left.

Turning, Sarah saw the widow. Miriam. She was looking over at Elsa and nodding in approval.

"Subtlety," she said.

"It sure is," said Sadie. "Miriam, this is Sarah Fisher, my best friend. Sarah, Mrs. Miriam Stolzfus."

"Nice to meet you," Sarah said automatically.

Now that she had the chance to see Miriam up close, she realized that she was not quite that young. There were a few lines around her eyes and mouth; her hair, though mostly dark, was shot through with a silvery gray. She was still beautiful, though.

"Oh, Sarah," said Miriam, smiling. "Your father has mentioned you."

Sarah blinked. Her father had mentioned her?

"Really?" she said.

"Yes. It was good to hear how great a help you've been to him after your family's losses." Miriam smiled sadly. "I wish I could have had such support. It's really wonderful."

Miriam's words sank in slowly. There was a brief pause, in which Sarah guessed she should say something – but she could not make a sound.

After a moment, Sadie stepped in. "Yes, Sarah and her *daed* are very close," she said.

Miriam nodded, still holding her soft, sad smile in place, before moving on.

Sarah stared after her as she moved away.

Her father had been talking about her to this woman? And not only that – not only that – he had spoken of their losses. *Losses,* plural. Meaning that he had not only talked of his wife's death with someone who was almost a complete stranger, when he barely even talked to Sarah about it, but he had also spoken of Mary.

Mary, whose name had not passed in their conversation since her funeral four years ago. Who had not even been mentioned by Sarah's *mamme* on her deathbed.

*What is going on?* wondered Sarah, though she did not speak the question aloud. Some small part of her realized that she already knew the answer.

Later still, when she and John were driving home, Sarah still would not let herself answer the question. Even when she noticed, again, how her father was looking up at the sky, the way she remembered him doing when she was little, and he would point out cloud shapes to her and Mary.

Not even when he asked her, in a falsely casual manner, whether she had met the newcomer.

"She's very nice," said Sarah, trying to ignore the way her chest suddenly felt cold, as though she were slowly filling with iced water.

*****

"He didn't *tell* you?"

Sadie seemed incredulous. Sarah supposed that with her big, loud family, always in each others' pockets, the idea of keeping any kind of secret was unthinkable.

"No," she said, opening the door of the gas powered refrigerator and pulling out two jugs of cold tea. "You're sure you saw them together?"

Not that Sarah had needed a confirmation. Her father had continued to find things "wrong" with the widow's cottage, going back week after week for the past month.

"Two days ago," affirmed Sadie, shutting the refrigerator door. "Walking together at sunset, down by the river."

"I see." Sarah placed the jugs on the table and started arranging the plates of cookies. "Well, he probably didn't want to say anything unless he thought – "

*It might lead to marriage.*

"Unless he thought something could happen," she said.

"In case he upset you?" asked Sadie.

"Maybe," said Sarah. She listened carefully to the women talking outside.

A group had come over to help her with her canning, the way they did every year. This year, the newcomer had been invited along as well; of course she had, it would have been strange otherwise. Sarah had been trying not to speak directly to Miriam, just in case she gave something away. The last thing she needed was for the women to come in and catch her and Sadie talking about this.

"*Are* you upset?" pressed Sadie.

"No..." said Sarah slowly. "Not that he might want to get married. That's to be expected."

Though she had not expected it. Not from the man who had spent the last three years staring at the floor, and talking only to her.

"I'm just not sure about *her.*"

"Miriam? What's wrong with her?" asked Sadie.

"I don't know. I'm not sure I trust her. We don't know anything about her, really."

"What's to know?" said Sadie, surveying the finished table. "Her husband passed away, she lived with her brother, then he got married and she moved out here."

"But where did she move from?" asked Sarah. "Who's this brother she decided to leave behind so suddenly? And why did she move at all – could she really not stand sharing a house with another woman? Why start from scratch? Why cut yourself off from all your friends and family, and live among strangers?"

"She moved from Green River in Indiana," said Sadie matter-of-factly. "And her brother's name is Jay. As to why she moved, you could always ask her."

"What makes you think she'd tell me the truth?" asked Sarah.

Sadie stared at her. "When did you become so skeptical?" she asked.

They were interrupted by one of the women – an older woman named Barbara, who was not known for her patience, putting her head through the kitchen door and asking if they were ready.

"Ready," said Sarah. "Come on in for refreshments!"

She ignored Sadie, who was still looking at her as though expecting an answer. What could she say? She knew that her emotions might well be affecting her judgment, but she could swear there was something about Miriam that was... off.

When the women entered and sat, Sarah was greatly displeased to find that Miriam took the seat right next to hers.

"Thank you again, everyone, for coming over," she said, hoping to keep the conversation general by addressing the table at large, rather than having to speak directly to her neighbor.

There was a general chorus of "of course, no trouble, you'd do the same for us."

"Sarah is a wonderful housekeeper," said Barbara, leaning over to Miriam.

"I can see that," smiled Miriam, glancing around the spotless kitchen.

"Been taking care of it all herself since she was fourteen, isn't that right, Sarah?"

Sarah looked down at her glass of tea.

"That's wonderful," said Miriam.

*No it isn't*, Sarah wanted to shout. How could Miriam of all people not understand what that meant?

Sarah's domain over the kitchen had been bestowed when her mother had fallen ill. Or, no, even before that; after Mary had died, *mamme* had struggled to manage her work. With no other siblings, Sarah had taken on as much as she could to save her mother trouble.

She had assumed, at the time, that her mother would take the reigns back as soon as she was able. But the diagnosis had come first.

The conversation returned to safer waters for a while, as everyone started talking about all the canning they needed to get done before the end of summer. Miriam was very interested to hear that there would be a market in early fall – she was having to buy everything at the moment, as her vegetable garden would not be ready for any sort of harvest this year.

"Will you be selling any of today's cherries?" she asked Sarah.

Sarah simply nodded, allowing the conversation to pass by her.

"Her sour cherries are even better," said someone down the table. "We did those a month ago."

"My husband can't get enough of sour cherry pie," said someone else. "I think he'd live on it if he were able."

"I always preferred the sour cherries to the sweet myself," said Miriam, smiling. "My husband was the one with the sweet tooth. One of the few things we ever disagreed on."

There were sympathetic nods up and down the table.

"Loss is a hard thing to bear," was Barbara's brilliant and insightful comment, as she looked at Miriam and then at Sarah.

Miriam nodded, and glanced at Sarah. Sarah flushed. The widow clearly thought they were having some kind of moment. She knew they she should say something, but she just couldn't bring herself to. What was it about Miriam that kept leaving her tongue-tied?

As the conversation finally moved on once more, Sarah did her best to avoid Sadie's still-questioning gaze; Sadie would have considered that moment a chance to open up to Miriam. Sarah did not know how to explain to her friend how necessary it was to hide her heart. She and John had both locked theirs away years ago.

It had been hard enough dealing with the suddenness of Mary's death.. Her death was the first tragedy Sarah had ever experienced, and she was completely unprepared. She had never known anyone who had died before, and had no context for the sudden, shattering blow and the gaping hole it left behind.

They had barely begun to deal with it when *mamme* had become ill. At that point, Sarah accepted every day as a continuation of some bad dream. After the diagnosis, the cancer had swept in with speed and without mercy, leaving them breathless and stunned when *mamme* had passed not three months after that first trip to the doctor.

She and John had dealt with their grief separately, as the idea of holding someone else's feelings as well as their own had seemed impossibly overwhelming. They had wrapped themselves up, and hidden away.

And now John was re-emerging. And Sarah had been left behind.

Was that why she was feeling this way? Maybe it was nothing to do with Miriam.

Maybe she was being selfish.

*I should try,* thought Sarah. *If I try to get to know her, reach out a little... at least if I learn more about her, then I can know for sure if there's anything to worry about, or if it's just me.*

*Yes, that's an idea.*

And so, as the canning party broke up later that afternoon and everyone started heading home, Sarah quickly ran down to the cellar and grabbed a jar of her sour cherries.

Running back upstairs, she spotted Sadie and Miriam about to leave, and waved at them to wait. Without giving herself time to hesitate, she walked over, pretending that she could not see Sadie looking worried.

"These are for you," she said, to Miriam, proffering the jar. "Sour cherries, to get your winter stock started."

Miriam took it, looking delighted. "That's so sweet of you," she said. "I really do love these in a pie."

"They're my favorites, too," Sarah said, feeling as though she was making a great concession in sharing personal information with Miriam.

"I'll try to make these last," Miriam said, still smiling. "They always got eaten up so quickly at home. This was really very nice of you, Sarah. If I stay long enough at the cottage, I'll hopefully have a harvest to pay you back with."

And then she and Sadie left, and Sadie looked behind her as she walked, communicating her approval at the effort Sarah had made. And Sarah stared after them.

*What did she just say?*

She went though it again in her head. Slowly, so as to be sure she was not making a mistake.

*No, I heard right,* she thought.

*But what does that mean?*

***

"*Daed?*"

"Hmm?" John looked over at his daughter. "What is it?"

Sarah looked down at her lap and nervously twitched the apron she was mending. She had brought it out to the porch, joining her father as he sat. But she had not been able to make a single stitch as she had thought about how to speak with him.

He was sitting to the side, looking out at the view taking in the sunset. It was certainly worth looking at, as the bright yellow clouds slowly singed themselves into red and the corn fields' gold deepened as though they were catching fire.

Sarah could not remember the last time she had seen John look so at peace.

And she had to break it.

"Ah – well, *daed*, you know Miriam – "

As she had feared, John immediately tensed.

"What about her?" he asked.

*Well, what about her,* Sarah thought, hesitating.

This was the problem; she did not have anything set in stone that she could tell her father. No evidence. Wouldn't he assume, as Sadie had, that Sarah was simply angry at the idea of her mother being replaced? He might think that she was upset he had kept his courtship of Miriam a secret from her.

John looked guilty already. Flustered.

Sarah wondered when she had last seen so many emotions play out across his face.

Not when *mamme* died. He had already shut himself away by then. For just a moment, Sarah did feel angry, really angry, that her father had withdrawn from his wife, and her, his daughter, and that he had needed some beautiful stranger to come and wake him from his slumber. She wanted to lash out and hurt him so that he would go back into hiding where he belonged, where she still was.

But no. She could not hold such dark thoughts in her heart. She loved her father. She knew he loved her, and that he may well love Miriam.

How could she do this to him?

And what if she was wrong?

A memory rose, unbidden. The last time Sarah had seen her father become emotional – really, truly, emotional, allowing himself to be so.

The day of Mary's death. She had heard him, from where he had been working with *mamme* in the kitchen. He had been screaming. *No, no, no.*

Sarah had rushed outside, pausing in the yard for just a moment to listen for where the sound was coming from. The barn, she had realized, and had begun to run towards it, calling out to John, asking what had happened. *I'm coming, daed.*

He had met her at the doorway of the barn. Stopped her, arms outstretched, pushing backwards and trying to shield her from getting a better look at the sight she had just managed to glimpse: a crumpled figure, lying awkwardly beneath the hole to the hay loft, the thin layer of straw on the ground around it stained dark.

*There's been an accident*, he had said. *Go up and tell your mamme, I'm right behind.* He had waited to tell her the truth. Protected her. She would do the same for him.

"I gave her some of our cherries," said Sarah. She picked up her needle and began working on the apron, keeping her gaze fixed downward as carefully as though she had never mended anything in her life before.

"That was nice of you," said John cautiously.

*What a fine family we are*, Sarah thought, her heart aching. *Sitting here and deceiving each other.*

"She was so pleased with them, I wished I'd given her a second jar," she continued. "I thought maybe if you were going back to work on the cottage, you might take one over?"

John nodded, as though it did not really matter one way or the other. "Sure," he said.

Sarah did not speak again, her eyes on her mending and her mind on what she would have to do.

She had an idea.

***

"How much longer do you think you'll be?"

Sarah looked up from her search.

"Sorry, Tom," she said. "I'm not sure... hopefully not long."

She looked over at Sadie, who was leaning against the wall next to a display of postcards with her eyes closed.

"Can't you lend a hand?" she called over.

"First of all," said Sadie, holding up one finger without opening her eyes, "I am still feeling sick from that car ride. I don't know how you spend all day in that thing, Tom."

"You get used to it," said Tom, rolling his eyes. It was a gesture that seemed oddly young for a man in his sixties.

Sadie held up another finger. "And second, I think what you're doing is insane, and I do not want to help you."

"Then why did you come?" asked Sarah, going back to looking through the bookshelves.

"Because whenever you utter the words 'I have an idea' I know that whatever follows is unavoidable," said Sadie. "All I can do is follow and make sure you don't do anything too crazy."

"She's got a point," said Tom.

"Why don't you get a cup of coffee, Tom?" suggested Sarah, pretending she had not heard either of them. "I'll pay."

"Nah," said Tom. "I've got a thermos in the car. Besides, the fare out here and back's going to cost you enough as it is... why don't I help you look? Which one is it again?"

"Green River," said Sarah. "Indiana."

Tom joined her at the bookshelf and started sorting through the directories.

Sarah was grateful that she knew Tom so well; she couldn't imagine most drivers would be willing to do this. Tom had taken the family up to the hospital and back several times during *mamme's* illness, and had become friendly with all of them. When he learned how serious the situation really was, he had given the family his personal number and told them to call any time they needed a ride. His mother had passed away from cancer too, he had said.

Tom had been the one to take them on that last trip to see *mamme*, and had bought Sarah a hot chocolate to drink on the way home, telling her sweetness was good for shock. Sarah had not seen him since then, as she had never needed a car, but he had remembered her as soon as she had called early this morning.

He had not even blinked when she had explained why she needed to be driven to the "Amish Gift Shoppe" over an hour away in Willow Grove.

Although he had pointed out that he had never had a request from an Amish person to go to the tourist shop unless they had a job there or were selling something. This was true enough – most of the people that Sarah knew tolerated these gift shops as a chance to sell crafts and cookery, but otherwise found them annoying. Sarah had only ever been in here once before, to arrange the sale of some of the crafts and canned goods left over from the yearly market.

She remembered seeing the assortment of directories and wondering why on earth they were selling such things in a gift shop. As though tourists had any right to peruse those pages and learn the names and ages of those who lived in the communities – for which the directories had actually been printed.

But now, she was grateful. Because not only did the shop sell directories, it boasted "directories of every Amish community in a thousand square miles (three for the price of two)". Which was exactly what she needed.

And, hopefully – *yes*. There it was.

"Got it," said Sarah. "Green River."

Sarah wanted to start looking through the booklet immediately, but the teen at the counter had been giving the group strange looks for the past few minutes. She would have to wait until she got home.

"So this is the clue you needed?" asked Tom, leaning against the counter as Sarah paid for the booklet. "To find out if this widow is lying?"

"I guess. I mean, I don't *want* her to be lying. I just... need to check. Could I have a bag for this?"

The teen grunted and disappeared into a stock room behind the counter.

"Fair enough," said Tom. "And how will the book help, if I can ask?"

"It lists the families that live in the community," explained Sarah. "Names, ages, and so on. Marriages and children."

"So you – what, you think she's lying about being married?"

"I think..." Sarah looked back down at the book. "I think she might have children."

Sarah could see Sadie shaking her head out of the corner of her eye. Sadie had already stated her opinion, multiple times, that Sarah was just looking for something to be wrong. That she wanted a reason for Miriam to be unsuitable.

But Sarah knew, she just *knew* that she was on to something.

And if Miriam did have children – if Sarah was right – then she had lied about it. And she had left them – where? And why? And who could tell, if she was lying about having children, then she might well still be married after all. She could have abandoned her family and come here, to start a new life. With John Fisher.

But Sarah would find out.

"Really," said Tom. "How'd you figure?"

"It was a few comments," said Sarah. "About children, and..." she hesitated. "And, well, cherries."

"Cherries," repeated Tom dubiously.

"I know how it sounds," said Sarah.

"And yet we're still here," came Sadie's voice from behind them.

Sarah shook her head and lapsed into silence and the teen reappeared with a brown paper bag for the booklet and a confused expression. Blushing, Sarah realized that their voices had probably carried into the stockroom.

When they reached home, Sarah had Tom drop her and Sadie off in a side road so they could walk home without being spotted. She nodded when he told her to say hi to her dad from him, although she knew that she could not say anything to her father about seeing Tom without having to explain what she had needed a car for.

Sarah and Sadie parted ways at the end of Sarah's lane.

"You didn't have to come, today," said Sarah. "But thank you all the same."

Sadie's face creased with sadness. "Oh, Sarah," she said, enveloping her friend in a hug. "I hope you're wrong, I really do."

"So do I," said Sarah, hoping fervently that she was telling the truth.

As soon as she reached the house, she settled herself at the kitchen table, poured a glass of water, took the booklet out of its bag, and began to leaf through it.

She almost wished, afterward, that it had taken her longer. Every moment before she knew the truth, she could keep herself in the space between knowing and unknowing. She did not have to face the part of herself that wanted Miriam to be guilty.

But the Plain community at Green River, Indiana, was not a large one, and the directory did not take long to read, so it only took a few minutes for Sarah to make her way through the entire thing without once reading the name "Miriam Stolzfus."

There was a Miriam Hoder, and a Miriam Mast. No Miriam Stolzfus.

Sarah checked the pages again, telling herself that she might have missed the name, all the while knowing that she had not missed it, and feeling a sickly rush of vindication, knowing that she had been right. Miriam had been lying.

And she, Sarah, was... happy about this? She did not want to be happy about this.

Turning back to her task, Sarah wondered whether Miriam might not have gone back to her maiden name, although that would be very unusual.

Sarah soon found one family named Stolzfus, but it was an elderly couple with two sons who had married an Esther and a Grace, and both new couples were in their early twenties.

She also looked for a Jay, Stolzfus or otherwise, but either Miriam had lied to Sadie about her brother's name or it was a nickname.

Would Miriam have even kept her first name? Sarah wondered. Or even told the truth about where she was from in the first place?

But she would probably have given something away if she was going by a false first name, like forgetting to answer when people addressed her directly. Miriam, Sarah knew now, was not very good at lying

It had been the cherries that had done it. Miriam had told Sarah that she always had requests for sour cherries at home. But before, she had told everyone that her husband did not like them. So who was making the requests?

It had not been quite enough by itself, but then Sarah had remembered the day she had met Miriam. The way she had looked at Sadie's mother with little Andrew, saying that she liked a similar approach herself. The way she had said it had made it sound, Sarah thought, as though she herself had children.

And now this.

Sarah went back to the two Miriams she had found. Which would it be? They were both married – the directory had been printed two years ago, and would not have recorded the death of Miriam's husband which, according to Sadie, had occurred only one year ago. Unless that was also a lie.

So. Miriam Mast had a young daughter, and a twelve year old son. She herself was in her early thirties. Two young to be the Miriam Sarah knew, surely? *Although some people do go gray early...*

But then she looked at Miriam Hoder. Forty years old, married to David Hoder, with three children. Sister of... James Lapp.

"*Jay*," whispered Sarah.

This was her. This was Miriam.

Three children... David Jr., fifteen years old, Isaac, eleven, and Peter, six.

She did have children.

And... she had left them behind?

*Why?*

"Why would she leave you?" Sarah murmured, staring at the page as though the images of the boys themselves would appear in her mind's eye.

"I thought it best," came a soft voice from behind her.

Sarah jumped, knocking her water glass onto the floor as she whipped around.

Miriam stood at the open back door, her expression shuttered, her posture bolt upright. She made no move to come inside.

Before she could say anything, Sarah heard footsteps in the hall.

"What was that?" John started to say as he entered – and then stopped, when he saw Miriam.

He paused, mirroring Miriam's position in the opposite doorway. He looked from her to Sarah, and to the broken glass on the floor.

"Sarah?" he said uncertainly. "What – "

And then Miriam said the last thing Sarah would have expected her to: "She knows."

"What?" said John again.

"*What?*" echoed Sarah, shocked in her turn. She looked at John. "You know? About the children?"

"Miriam told me," said John, taking a compulsive step into the room and glancing at the as-yet unmoving figure of the widow herself. "How do *you* know?"

Sarah gestured at the directory on the table. Then she turned back to Miriam.

"No, wait," she said. "How did you know – that I knew?" She was too flustered to think of a better way to phrase the question.

"I was at the gift shop," said Miriam quietly. "In the stockroom. I heard you talking."

"What were you doing there?" asked Sarah, still feeling accusatory.

"I sell quilts," said Miriam.

Sarah could not think of anything to say to that, so she looked at her father. His gaze was still squarely on her. He did not look angry, not exactly. Sarah almost wished that he did, she felt as though she could do with an argument. Miriam was being entirely too calm.

"Sarah," said John gently. "Why didn't you just talk to me about this?"

Sarah narrowed her eyes slightly. "When did you give me a reason to?" she demanded. "How can I talk to you when you never talk to me?"

John flinched.

"I know you two are courting," Sarah went on. "I had to find out from *Sadie.* Who was so surprised that I didn't know, what with us being so close, and all each other has."

John bowed his head for a moment. "I'm sorry, Sarah. I was trying to... protect you, I guess."

Sarah bit her lip as he looked down.

"You were trying to protect each other."

Sarah looked over at Miriam, surprised to hear her chiming in. She nodded.

"I was trying to protect you, *daed,*" she said. "I didn't want to tell you what I suspected until I was sure. But I guess I wasted my time. You're the only one that *wasn't* being lied to."

She turned back to Miriam. "I'm glad my *daed* knows the truth, at least," she said. "Were you ever going to tell anyone else?"

Somehow, strangely, this exchange with her father had calmed Sarah. She did not feel so angry as she had before. As her thoughts cleared, she could see the sadness in Miriam's expression. And even though she knew now beyond a doubt that her suspicions had been correct, Sarah could not help but feel her heart going out to the widow.

"Ask her why," John prompted softly. "Why she sells quilts."

Sarah looked curiously at Miriam.

"I'm saving," she said. "I want to bring my boys out to live with me."

"And... why aren't they with you now?" asked Sarah.

The older woman sighed softly, and finally took a step into the kitchen.

"They're with my brother. He's shared legal guardianship with me since my husband died. I was living there too, but my brother is... unkind."

Miriam's eyes flicked downward, and she moved a hand up to her throat. As Sarah realized what Miriam meant, she felt her stomach drop slightly. She glanced at her father, whose jaw was set.

"He had been bad-tempered when we were growing up, but it was worse when I started keeping house for him. I thought I could deal with it, I didn't have anywhere else to go. But then the boys, they started to defend me. David, the oldest, especially. He got hurt."

Miriam clasped her hands tightly together.

"But Jay loved the boys, he never raised his voice to them once on their own account, let alone his hand. It was only when they got between him and me."

There was a pause.

"So you left," said Sarah softly.

"I've been trying to get money together so I can bring them over," said Miriam. "And I had to change my name so Jay wouldn't be able to find us. He'd take them back if he did, I wouldn't be able to fight him."

"But I suggested," said John, walking over to stand next to Miriam, "that if Miriam were to marry, the boys would become part of her husband's family."

He placed a hand on Miriam's shoulder; the two of them looked at Sarah, worry etched across their faces. They were waiting for her approval.

And, as the last of her anger fluttered away, Sarah nodded slowly.

"That... seems like a good solution," she said.

She saw both her father and Miriam visibly relax. John smiled at Miriam; a warm, wide smile. Miriam blushed as though she were Sarah's age. They really did love each other, Sarah realized. Even without the problem of Miriam's children, they would have been married. Of course they would.

"So you'll be married in Fall," said Sarah. A troubling thought struck her. "But then you won't be able to fetch the boys until November at the earliest."

She thought, perhaps, that she should slow down and process everything, before looking to solve any more problems.

But then, what was there to process? Her father would remarry. And she would get to know Miriam – and the boys, when they got here – and they would become a family.

It was not a future that Sarah would have been able to recognize before this moment, but it was one she thought she could soon learn to love.

"That's months without seeing them," she said. "How long since you saw them last?"

"A week before I arrived here," said Miriam, her voice shaking almost imperceptibly. "I call David once a week from the tourist shop – he sneaks out to the neighbor's barn, they've a phone in there – since I left, Jay's kept such a close eye on them, that's all the contact we can manage."

Sarah looked at her father – and considered, for a moment, how she would feel in that situation.

Then: "I have an idea," she said.

***

Sarah ran to the driver's side door and knocked on the glass.

"Tom," she panted, as he rolled down the window, "they've found a gap in the hedge behind the house, it's out of sight of the yard. Can you reverse back around that corner?"

Tom looked back at where she was pointing and rolled his eyes.

"I can turn around and drive forward around the corner," he said. "Whoever heard of reversing around a corner? And even if I did, I wouldn't do it in a minivan. Honestly, you're lucky I agreed to drive this thing at all."

Sarah just nodded, knowing that he did not expect an answer. She paused for a moment, peering over the tall board fence to see if her father was managing to distract Jay. Yes, it looked like they were still talking. John had agreed to pretend that he was lost and needed directions, and Miriam had provided him with a list of topics to use to keep the conversation going.

Sarah started back the way she had come, to where Miriam was helping the boys to make their way quietly across the back yard and through the gap in the hedge.

She was interrupted by Tom calling after her.

"Tell them to bring snacks if they want," he said. "I'm not stopping once we're off, just in case whats-his-name calls the cops. I've got some chocolate if they're desperate."

"Sure," said Sarah.

And despite Tom's worries, she could not bring herself to be concerned. She knew in her heart that they would make it. She had said as much to Miriam during the long drive here in the early hours of the morning. They had held hands in the gray dawn, and Sarah had promised that this would work. Of course it would. It had been her idea, after all.

She smiled as she ran back toward her new family.

# AN AMISH FRIENDSHIP

## ERICA FANNING

Living in the Plain community was an absolute joy. In the spring and summer, there were parties and get-togethers in the town square. Young love was in the air and many weddings were conducted. In the fall was the harvest time, where the community would come together as always and help everyone to make sure nothing was left unharvested. Much of what was made and harvested was sold on market days to Englishers passing through from one big city to another. What wasn't sold was saved and stored for the community and for each respective family to help them through the harsh winter. Being in the northeastern part of the country made each winter unpredictable, but they always made their way through it and began to prepare for as many contingencies as possible.

No one could prepare for the contingency of what was about to come upon them.

Rebecca Miller did her usual winter morning duties before the rest of the family was up: feeding the chickens, gathering their eggs, and making sure they were warm. She also checked the garden one last time. It hadn't snowed yet this year, but the ominous clouds above her head and the cold north wind threatened it at any moment. She pulled the shawl she was wearing a little tighter and noticed that there were a few extra vegetables her little brother had missed in his excitement over the stray dog in their yard yesterday. She smiled remembering his little face light up as he ran toward the strange creature. Rebecca's father, Joseph Miller, wouldn't allow the family to get a dog unless they could find one with the right temperament to guard the chickens. Little Matthew was bound and determined that the dog he found was the one.

"I don't think that's how it works, buddy," Rebecca had said. "Besides, this one has a rope around his neck. He probably belongs to someone." Rebecca wasn't going to mention to Matthew that the bullmastiff's massive head gave her some unease. *That thing could eat you alive,* is what she had wanted to say, but instead she went with,

"Let's get you inside. If he's still here when we're done with snack, then we'll talk to Papa about keeping him."

Matthew had been disappointed, but he agreed.

Today, the silence in the air made it seem like not another soul on the earth even existed. Any moment now, it was going to snow. Rebecca hurried inside and no sooner had she walked inside and the snow slowly began falling.

Rebecca loved the snow, it always gave the earth a sort of "do-over" look. She watched it for a few moments before realizing her arms were full of vegetables and eggs. She watched the snow a few seconds more, and then went about her chores for the day.

By mid-afternoon, the snow had been falling steadily now. Matthew was more than excited and wanted to go play with his friends. Papa wouldn't allow it because the Miller's didn't have proper winter attire.

"I don't need you getting sick, my son."

Only three winters ago, Mary Miller, their beloved wife and mother, passed away from pneumonia. Rebecca wasn't above taking her into the nearest town to get medical help, but Papa strictly forbade it.

"No," he had said. "The Miller's haven't been to an English community in over a hundred and fifty years. We're not about to start now. God will heal your Mama."

Both Rebecca and Matthew—who had only been 8 at the time—were scarred toward God and anything taught in church for a long time. Since Matthew was younger, he was able to accept that maybe God allowed it to happen because of some hidden sin that he didn't know about. Rebecca knew better. A loving God wouldn't allow any of His children to be harmed like that. He wouldn't allow a woman who loved Him almost as much as King David in the Bible to be brought down with one of the worst illnesses known to the Plain community. No, she decided she would stay within the community for her little brother, but she wouldn't really serve this supposed God that caused her mother to die.

In fact, most of the time, snow caused her to think very fondly of her mother and how much she loved snow. When it snowed, it was hard for Rebecca to think anything ill toward anyone. She smiled at Matthew trying to convince her to help change Papa's mind.

"Silly boy," she laughed. "You're not going to be able to convince him to let you out. Maybe in the springtime, we'll start making winter clothing so you can go play with your friends next year."

"But that's next year," Matthew pouted. "Maybe James' family has something extra. Please, Rebecca? Can't we at least go ask?"

Rebecca sighed and looked at her father who was standing in the doorway of the living room, where his two children were. He nodded once. She smiled at her little brother. "Let's go."

As soon as Rebecca set a booted foot outside the front door, she knew this snow wasn't going to let up anytime soon. In fact, in the short amount of time it took her and Matthew to get to their neighbors, there was already another quarter of an inch of snow on the ground. As soon as Naphtali Fisher saw the young Miller's out in the snow, she ran outside and covered them both in an extra shawl.

"What do you two think you're doing?" She scolded them as soon as they were inside. "This snow is accumulating so quickly, and Matthew is so little he could get stuck!"

"Mrs. Fisher, I want to play outside with James," Matthew announced as if Naphtali hadn't said anything. "Do you have any extra winter clothes for me?" He looked at her waiting, as she looked at Rebecca in disbelief.

"You came all the way here so he could ask to play out in this?" She looked at Matthew. "No, dear. James is sick. He has the flu. I don't want you to get sick either; maybe you should stay here with us."

"Oh no," Rebecca interjected before Matthew could say anything. "If there's someone sick here, it might be better if we head back. Besides, Papa would be worried for us. Thank you."

Naphtali insisted they take the extra shawls and simply return them when they could. Naphtali was a seamstress by trade and by hobby. Their house was never short of clothing or anything made of fabric.

"You mustn't go by yourselves," Mrs. Fisher insisted one last time. "Luke!" She called for her oldest son and he came around the corner in a flash.

"Yes, Mama?" It had been months since Rebecca had seen Luke Fisher, but she didn't remember him being that handsome. He was well-toned in his body, and he had a lean face with gentle brown eyes underneath a full head of wavy brown hair.

It took Rebecca a moment to realize she had stopped breathing. She knew Mrs. Fisher and Matthew were both talking to her, but she simply remembered walking out the door and it wasn't until they were halfway home that she realized Luke was right there next to her, guiding her steps and making small talk. She knew she was responding, but couldn't remember any of the conversation they had. She did remember him wishing her a goodnight and telling her he would see her in the morning at church.

*Church?* She didn't realize tomorrow was a church day. "Papa, there's church tomorrow?"

Papa laughed. "I would hope so, my dear. It's Sunday. I know it's not too late, but would you go check on the chickens one last time before it gets too dark?"

Rebecca obeyed, and while she was out there, she tried desperately to remember what she and Luke had talked about on the way home, but all she was coming up with was the way his voice sounded and how steady his hands were whenever she lost her balance. It wasn't until today that she realized having a mate in her life would be an amazing experience, and she hoped that it would be Luke. She was only 16, but she knew she was ready for marriage because that's what the Plain community taught its young women to be prepared for. Rebecca had mastered much of what her mother had taught her in the three years since she had left this earth.

She decided staying outside with the chickens much longer was a bad idea because the wind began to pick up and kick a lot of the snow about. She locked the pen up tightly so the door wouldn't fly open with the wind and quickly returned inside.

"Papa, the weather's starting to get really bad outside. Do you think they'll even had church tomorrow?" Rebecca didn't want to try to travel in this weather if she could avoid it.

"Well, if they ring the bell, then we'll know." The bell was used to assemble the churchgoers, but in extreme cases like this, it was used as a warning to stay where they were. But no sooner had he finished speaking and the church bell rung.

"Quickly! Get as much as you can: food, blankets, clothing. We're going to the church."

The snow was so deep, Matthew kept getting stuck. Papa finally had to carry him to the church. When they arrived, it was already almost full to the brim of people who lived closer than the Miller's.

"How are they going to fit everyone in here?" Rebecca asked absently. Just then Luke Fisher came up to them.

"The basement is open for those who are sick. We still plan on having church in the morning, but we might just move the pews tonight to make room for makeshift beds. Mr. Miller, the men are meeting on the stage to talk about a plan. Would you be willing to help us?"

Papa looked at Rebecca and she nodded. She would stay with Matthew while he helped the men.

"Come, Matthew. Let's get out of the doorway." Rebecca moved them to a warm spot in the sanctuary. There were already a lot of people there, but Rebecca knew they were going to have to get cozy if they wanted to stay alive.

"Excuse me everyone!" It was Luke. Rebecca wasn't sure where the preacher was, but people seemed to listen to Luke just as well. It became quiet except for the people that were still coming in. "Thank you all for coming. Preacher Hostetler has informed me that they are predicting this weather to be some of the worst we've seen in over a hundred years." There were murmurs in the crowd. People were getting nervous.

"There's no need to worry. We have a food stash in the cellar and it looks like some of the other women of the community have brought their own food. We won't ask you to share, but if you want to do so, anything you can give to the community would be greatly appreciated.

"Now, we're still figuring out the logistics of how we're going to bed everyone in here. We want to keep the basement for those who are sick, but we will need volunteers to help care for them. If that's something you want to do, please come stand to the left of the stage."

Rebecca knew in her heart that's what she wanted to do, but she couldn't leave Matthew all alone. She looked at her father, who was standing within visual range, and she caught his eye. He glanced at the growing throng of women, then looked at her and cocked his head. He was okay with her going as long as Matthew stayed put.

"Matthew, I need you to stay here with Miss Mary." The young schoolteacher had been sitting there and had seen the exchange between Rebecca and her father.

"Don't worry about him. He'll be fine," she assured her. Rebecca thanked her and hurried over with the group. As soon as she got over there, Luke announced that they had an ample amount of women and would need others to help cook for the healthy.

"With this many people, it's going to take community effort to make sure we all get out of this alive." Luke continued giving directions for a few more minutes and then dismissed everyone to go to their stations.

Mrs. Stoltzfus was the oldest woman in the group of caretakers, so she quickly took charge and began ordering everyone about as soon as they got to the basement. Since it was late in the evening, they were simply trying to make sure that the sick were comfortable and then began making arrangements for food to be brought down as soon as possible. Rebecca was the youngest of the caretakers, so she did a lot of the running up and down the stairs to make sure the communication stayed open between the floors and the leaders. Basically, she became the messenger girl. She didn't mind so much because that gave her an excuse to see Luke more often and even to talk to him.

By midnight, Rebecca was exhausted and just wanted to sleep. Mrs. Stoltzfus noticed her fatigue and sent her upstairs to sleep with her family. She didn't argue and was glad for the short respite.

When Rebecca woke up the next morning, her throat was on fire and she felt dizzy. She thought nothing of it as she took a swig of some water, washed her face, and hurried downstairs to help. It felt cooler than she remembered and her body shivered. As soon as Mrs. Stoltzfus saw her, she made her sit down.

"Child, you don't look well." The older woman felt Rebecca's forehead. "In fact, you have a fever. Here, we have an extra bed for you right next to James Fisher." Mrs. Stoltzfus led her to the bed and helped her lie down. "I might need your help, but I do believe you're coming down with the flu. It would be best if you stayed still and let the fever pass."

"No, Mrs. Stoltzfus," Rebecca tried to argue. "I'm fine. I think it's just because I didn't sleep well last night. I'll be fine." Mrs. Stoltzfus pushed her down.

"No, child," she insisted. "You stay right there." She helped Rebecca take her shoes off and pulled a blanket up to her chin. "If I see you get up, I will tie you down to this bed."

James Fisher snickered at that. "Oooh, Rebecca's in trouble." He laughed again which led to a coughing fit.

"Now, now," Mrs. Stoltzfus turned from Rebecca to focus on James' coughing. "You must be careful child. Here," she handed him some herbal tea that had been by his bed. "Drink this and your throat will feel better."

"But it's cold."

"I'll go make you some new tea while I cook some up for Miss Miller." She scurried off, making sure to tell some of the other caretakers to keep an eye on Rebecca and James as she went to make more tea.

Rebecca sat up as soon as she was out of sight and kicked the blanket off. "I can't stay here."

"Heh, well don't let Mrs. Stoltzfus find out you're getting up," a voice behind her stated. She spun around to see James' oldest brother Luke standing there, arms folded. "She seemed pretty serious about tying you to the bed."

"You heard that?" Rebecca asked quietly. Luke laughed and nodded as her face flushed. James laughed with his brother.

"Actually, she had to tie me down too, and I've been sick for a week." James seemed very excited about this. "But I know I'm getting better. I already feel like I could run a race!"

Luke went over to his brother's bed and sat on it. "That's great, but you know Mrs. Stoltzfus won't let you go until we can get an actual doctor in here to make sure you're alright."

"Wait," Rebecca stopped him. "We're having an actual doctor come in?" Luke sighed sadly.

"There's almost two feet of snow outside. I don't think anyone's coming for a few days... but last night Mrs. Stoltzfus asked me if I would call a doctor in so that we don't lose people to simple illnesses that the English medical community has found cures for." He lowered his voice before adding, "Like your mother."

Rebecca felt her chest tighten. All those questions of why's and what if's suddenly came back and flooded her thoughts. Suddenly she couldn't catch her breath. Luke had laid her down and was standing over her. He was yelling something, but all she could hear was the quickening sound of her heart, struggling to get oxygen to her brain. The edges of Rebecca's vision began to blur just as Mrs. Stoltzfus came up and sat her up. She was telling her to breathe. She began counting: 1, 2, 3, 4,... The feeling passed as quickly as it came.

"Good job," Mrs. Stoltzfus smiled calmly. "Take a few deep breaths slowly. Do you feel alright now?" Rebecca nodded slowly.

"Rebecca, I am so sorry," Luke said apologetically. "I had no intention of hurting you—"

"Stop." Rebecca didn't want to hear it right now. She just wanted to sleep. She began to lie back, but Mrs. Stoltzfus kept her sitting up.

"You have to drink this first." She handed Rebecca the herbal tea with lemon and honey. Rebecca took a few sips and thanked the woman, who looked at Luke and told him sternly it was time to leave.

Luke looked defeated and helpless, but wasn't about to argue. Slowly, he walked toward the stairs and out of sight.

"Whatever he said to you, honey, don't let it affect you." Mrs. Stoltzfus placed her hand gently on Rebecca's arm. "Sometimes people don't understand what it's like to lose someone they love. He didn't mean anything he said in a harsh way." Rebecca nodded.

"I know," she responded quietly. "It wasn't what he said, but the thoughts that came with it. What happened to me?" The lead caretaker smiled warmly.

"Something we're going to avoid from happening ever again."

As the days went on, some of the younger sick ones began to get better, James and Rebecca among those. As soon as Rebecca was better, she began helping as a caretaker again. She needed something to do to keep her mind off of the fact that they were still stuck in the church. It had been five days and the snow still hadn't let up. Some of the snowbanks were well over ten feet tall and the church doors had been snowed in by day two of the storms. Thankfully the entire community had managed to fit well into the little church place, but many of them were beginning to wonder why they hadn't seen the preacher or his family. Rumors had begun flying that they had gotten stuck in the parish next door. They saw lights on every night from what little could be seen out the windows.

Every night the community got together to pray for the preacher, for the county, for the community's animals that had been left unattended and even for the surrounding English communities. Perhaps they had amenities that the Plain community didn't, but as Luke pointed out during prayer one night, they were still struggling with the same elements and they didn't prepare every year like the community did.

Although Rebecca had been upset by what Luke had said, she also saw how hurt he was by what he had said. She made it a point to go out of her way to talk to him one day during lunch.

"May I sit with you?" She asked politely after she found him sitting alone. He looked up and nodded, his mind seemingly somewhere else. "Are you alright?"

"No," he finally admitted. "The preacher... I know where he is, and it's not next door." Rebecca waited for more, but finally had to ask him to elaborate. "The preacher is the one that went to get a doctor to come look at the sick. I haven't heard from him or anyone, and the cellular phone he provided hasn't had service in three days. I don't want to be depressing, but I don't think he's even alive." He looked up at Rebecca and she saw that he had tears in his eyes. "I'm afraid, Rebecca."

She moved around to his side of the table and held him as he began to cry. The sat like that for a long time before someone called Luke's name. He quickly sat up and wiped his face.

"I have to go."

"I understand." Rebecca was upset that she wasn't able to talk to him, but she knew in her heart that she had forgiven him.

"Thank you," he said as he looked into her eyes, fresh tears welling up. "I feel like I can trust you, and I have always appreciated that about you, Rebecca Miller." He got up and left her sitting there alone.

She knew in her heart that she would never forget this moment... and she would never tell anyone where the preacher really was. She sent up a quick prayer for his safety and hoped he'd made it to town before the storm had gotten too bad, but like Luke she felt in her heart that it was probably too late for him. And that would be the most painful thing for the community to accept.

The next morning, the snow had finally stopped and the sun was shining. It helped to heat the little church some, since there was still so much snow on the windows. The community was abuzz with excitement about how soon they might be able to leave and get back to their abodes to assess the damage. Luke assured everyone that as soon as they could dig their way out of the church and onto the road, people could begin leaving. They were going to have to stay in the church a few more days before that happened though. The men were still putting a plan together on what the next steps were to be.

Indeed, it was another five cold days in the church before the men began to dig a way out of the church. The congregation cheered, and since Rebecca was downstairs helping with the sick, she was sent to see what was happening. The news brought so much hope into the room that many of the sick seemed to get better just by hearing it.

"We need to begin making preparations to leave as soon as possible," Mrs. Stoltzfus told Rebecca and another young girl. "Begin packing everything that we don't absolutely need—any extra bandages, extra tea, that sort of thing. Quickly now!"

"Make way!"

Suddenly there was a hustling coming down the stairs and the three women were almost forced out of the way. There were two men—Luke and Mr. Miller—carrying someone between them... the preacher!

Without any more pleading, Rebecca and the other girl went and retrieved as many extra blankets as they could. The preacher—Troyer—was blue, but he was still breathing. He was wrapped in blankets of his own and had a hat and mittens on, but they didn't know how long he'd been outside.

A crowd had begun forming around the small bed and on the stairs as people were clamoring to see their beloved preacher. Mrs. Stoltzfus shooed them all away with a word and went back to peeling the frozen clothes off of the preacher.

"Set up a curtain for us," she told Rebecca. "We don't need prying eyes to see what our beloved preacher is going through." She ran off to find Naphtali Fisher, the seamstress. She had brought a whole bag of extra blankets and shawls. Maybe she had something to use as curtains.

She found the woman upstairs helping Miss Mary corral the children away from the door in an attempt to keep them warm. There were still men digging their way to the road... Rebecca wasn't sure why the door was still open. She asked them as soon as she reached them.

Naphtali hissed, "I'm not sure, but whoever left it open is about to receive the wrath of God." Rebecca almost forgot why she was there, but as soon as she remembered she spoke in quick sentences. Immediately Naphtali's countenance changed and she went to work finding as much material as she could to help Rebecca make the curtains she needed.

"God bless you child, and God help our preacher." She seemed on the verge of tears; apparently she had been one of the few who hadn't been informed of the new developments. Rebecca nodded and ran down the stairs and began setting up the curtains for more privacy. Mrs. Stoltzfus had the preacher almost completely undressed, and it didn't look good.

She wanted to know how long he had been out there, and where exactly "there" was. Why was he outside by himself? Why didn't he call for help? The questions began forming faster than she could stop them. Her chest began to tighten again and her vision became blurry.

Mrs. Stoltzfus caught it in time and said calmly but firmly, "Breathe, child." Rebecca began counting: *1, 2, 3, 4,...* She took a few deep breaths and hurriedly finished her task.

As soon as she finished, she ran back upstairs to find out why the door was still open. She couldn't find anyone to ask, but the sun on her skin felt nice and warm despite the chill of the winter air. She basked in it only a moment before closing the door firmly and making sure it would still be accessible and easy to open. Luke appeared as soon as she walked away from the door.

"Why did you close the door?" He seemed upset; under the circumstances, that was understandable.

"Because it's cold outside and we don't want the entire community to get sick."

"But we need it open so we can go in and out easily."

"If you need to keep a door open because of convenience, then you shouldn't be living here. There's an English town less than an hour away that will take your convenience. But here, you have to work a little harder to get what you want." Luke pulled back. Rebecca was shocked that even came out of her mouth. "I'm so sorry, I—"

"No," Luke pushed past her, nostrils flaring. "You're not." He slammed the door on his way out, causing those closest to the front of the church to focus their attention on Rebecca. She looked down and walked away as if nothing had happened, but inside she felt as if her world was falling apart. She had no idea how she could possibly have any feelings for Luke Fisher despite all of the things that had happened these past twelve days. She tried to push all of the thoughts out of her mind as she went back downstairs to help Mrs. Stoltzfus and the preacher.

Within a day, a snowplow from the English town had come through and cleared a lot of the snow off of the main road, making the possibility of going home closer than ever. Some people were anxious to what their homes would look like, others were concerned about the animals they'd hastily left behind, but there wasn't one soul who didn't first fear for the future of their preacher and what his fate would be.

A doctor from the English town also came the same day as the snowplow. Luke had managed to get signal on his cellular phone to call the hospital. When the doctor arrived, he immediately called for an ambulance.

"This man has extreme hypothermia. It is literally a miracle that he's still alive. How did this happen?"

Mr. Miller answered, "We found him stuck in a snowbank less than twenty feet outside the door. We don't even know how long he was there. Is he going to make it?"

The doctor shook his head. "I don't know. The damage seems too extensive. I'm not going to make any promises just yet."

Within a few days, they knew the answer. The preacher had passed on. The hypothermia had affected his internal organs too much and nothing they did would fix it.

Luke Fisher was most affected by this, next to the preacher's family. Luke had been mentored by the preacher and was hoping to one day be a preacher in a town of his own one day. Rebecca did what she could to console Luke, but ever since their episode at the church door, Luke had been distant.

With the passing of the preacher and the assessing of their community, everyone's spirits were down. Nearly all the farm animals survived, but the bullmastiff that Matthew had found wandering had died in a snowbank, forever lost to his owners. Matthew cried when Rebecca informed him.

"Why didn't the owners take him back?" There was little consoling the heart of an 11-year-old. Rebecca knew he would bounce back quickly.

There was a lot of damage to houses and to the schoolhouse. Even the church had sustained some damage. Luke took charge and rallied everyone together for one last supper before they officially returned to their homes to rebuild.

Rebecca felt that this would be the best time to try to talk to him before they were simply neighbors again. The way he had treated her for the past week had hurt her every single time she saw him.

"Luke," she began after she came up to the table he was seated at with the preacher's family. She nodded to them and apologized for their loss. "Can we talk in private?"

He didn't seem eager to talk, but he didn't say no. They found a quiet corner and she just let all of her feelings out.

"From the time you walked me home on the first day of snow, to the last argument we had... and everything in between, I've realized something." She stopped and looked away from his face, afraid that she wouldn't be able to finish if she had to look in his eyes for another second.

She continued, "You've been strong, courageous, bold, caring, and passionate. I... I was wondering how you would feel about us courting." She waited a moment before raising her eyes to meet his. She was shocked to see tears streaming down his face, which was soft and tender in that moment.

"Oh Rebecca," he spoke her name as if it was the greatest name in the world. "From the moment your brother became friends with mine, I knew this moment would come. I so desperately wanted you to love me, but was too afraid to do anything because you were going through such a hard time with..." he trailed off, probably afraid Rebecca would have one of her panic attacks. She nodded in understanding.

"Go on."

He moved closer to her, closing the already small gap between them. Her breathing became shallow, but not in the way it had in the past. This was a new feeling. What was this?

"Rebecca Miller," Luke stated, his face only inches from her. "I would love to court you." He kissed her lightly on the lips and a thousand butterflies went off in her stomach at that moment. As quickly as he kissed her, it was over, leaving Rebecca wanting so much more. Luke smiled, seeing the disappointment and confusion on her face.

"You're still only sixteen." He winked. "We'll work up to something better."

"You..." she didn't even know what to say, so she punched him playfully on the arm. He laughed.

"Come on, you should meet the Troyer's."

It was a wonderful thing to see the community come together in their time of mourning and rebuilding. They decided to work on the church and the parish first, since those were the most important buildings in the community. Then they moved onto different barns where the most food was stored. Luke had decided the plan of action would then include working on the houses of the older members of the community, and then those with the youngest children. If the community worked on one thing at the same time, it was accomplished a lot faster. Within two weeks, it was as if nothing had even ravaged the community.

Almost, anyway.

The community was still out a preacher, but the bishop had allowed Luke to preach until they could find a suitable preacher, the Troyer's had to find somewhere else to live, and the community was still mourning the death of their lost shepherd.

Joseph Miller allowed the Troyer's to live with them until a house could be built, so the house suddenly became very full. With Matthew and Rebecca, plus the three young Troyer children, there were five children under the age of 18. Ms. Troyer helped Rebecca with a lot of the cleaning and cooking duties, while Matthew would entertain the children. Mr. Miller was out fixing his barn and tending to his regular winter duties most of the day, so it gave the women some time to talk.

Rebecca could tell that Ms. Troyer was starting to become fond of her father and sometimes she even dropped hints to her Papa that such a thing was happening.

"Papa, you can't shrug this off forever. Mama would want you to be happy and live your life."

"But Rebecca, I am happy. I have my two wonderful children. What else could I need?" Rebecca knew that now was the time to tell him about her and Luke.

"Papa, I won't be here forever." He looked at her, concerned.

"Why?" She laughed.

"Well I'm not dying. Papa, Luke and I are courting! We could be married within the next year! With your permission, of course."

He looked at her for a moment before staring into his hands as if the answer would materialize.

"I don't know what to say," he spoke with a gruff voice. "But I know that I can't try to court someone whose husband has just died."

"But Papa, she's ready when you are." He narrowed his eyes at her.

"How do you know?"

"She talks about you all the time. It's been almost 2 months and she will need help with the children. You're not that much older than her, Papa. At least consider it."

The next night at dinner, there was a special announcement: Ms. Troyer and Mr. Miller were to begin courting, but slowly at first. Papa had decided that they could at least explore the possibility and the best way for that to happen was while they were in the same house together.

"I have a beautiful daughter that will keep me in check for the time being and a son who watches everything I do. I won't let you down." He smiled at Matthew and Rebecca.

The only thing left to do was see if Luke was still serious about courting. Rebecca had left him alone during the rebuilding of the community, but now that they were done and there was a new preacher in place, she knew this was the best time to talk to him.

She found him sitting at an old picnic table on the back side of the church. The weather had warmed up considerably and much of the snow that wasn't directly on the ground had melted. Rebecca joined him and decided to get right to it.

"Are we still going to court?" Luke was quiet for a while and Rebecca began to wonder if he had even heard her. She almost asked the question again until he answered.

"I think so."

"You think so?" He nodded.

"If we do this," they locked eyes, "this is it. I don't go around and 'try out' girls like some of the other guys do. It's either me, or it's the dating game." Rebecca wanted to answer quickly but realized that she needed to think about this. She was only 16 and if this was it, there would be no other. She stared at the table for a few minutes while she thought, but she knew her answer.

"This has always been it." She looked at him. "At the end of the day, it's always you and me, leading the way. We make sure our families are provided for and that everyone is safe. Why not do it together?"

"Wow," Luke said after a minute. "That was really poetic. Do you always talk like that?" Rebecca shrugged.

"I guess you bring the poet out in me."

"Either that, or I bring out a panic attack."

They laughed as Luke bent down and threw some snow in Rebecca's direction. This was truly the man she wanted to be with, and she knew that nothing else would be so important as this decision here and now. This beautiful friendship would turn into a beautiful romance... and that was the best thing for Rebecca and for her father. She was glad for this new stage in life and wanted nothing else than to enjoy this snowball fight with the man that would soon become her husband.

# Susan's Rumspringa

SABRINA VICKS

## Chapter 1

"Are you ready for tomorrow?" Susan's mother asked her as they sat together at the dining room table. Susan looked at her mother and twirled her cinnamon locks in between her fingers.

"I think so," she said nodding. "It's funny how you wait for this day to come for some many years and it seems so exciting, but now it has finally arrived and I am so nervous, I'm practically shaking."

"Rumspringa is a crucial time for the Amish youth, Susan. You will go out into the world beyond our community and you will get to experience and see things you have never thought were possible. It will be shocking, but it will also be fun for you." Susan's mother took her hand and gently brushed her fingers. "You have grown up so fast. It seems that it was only yesterday that you were a little girl, running in the fields and laughing with friends."

"Mother?" Susan asked, "Are you worried that I will choose to stay out there? Do you think I won't come back?"

Her mother smiled softly and shook her head, "Let's get some rest. Tomorrow will be a big day for both of us."

Susan went into her bedroom and closed the door behind her. She laid down in her bed and thoughts swirled in her mind about all of the possibilities the next couple of years might bring. She thought about the previous years and how she would watch parents saying goodbye to their children, but they almost always came back in the end. There were only a few times that she could think of where a person would decide to leave the church and try to make it out there in the world.

She could not understand what would compel a person to make that decision, but maybe she was about to find out.

***

Susan woke up in the morning earlier than usual. She could feel butterflies fluttering around her stomach as she sat up on her bed. She looked around the room and gave some quiet thanks for everything she'd been blessed with before standing up and getting dressed.

As she walked out of her room, she thought what a lovely surprise it would be for her mother if she made breakfast for her this morning. She made her way into the kitchen, and to her surprise, her mother was already in there stirring away.

"Mom?" Susan laughed, "You couldn't sleep either?"

"Not today! It's a big day for you and I wanted to make sure that you had enough food to keep you strong," her mother answered without looking up at Susan.

"It's alright, mom, it's only two years. It's not a lifetime!"

"Yes, well, let's pray that is the case." Her mother looked over her shoulder and flashed Susan a small smile. Susan went over to her side and the two of them finished preparing their meal in silence. As they sat down to take in their meal, they gave thanks to the Lord for His bounty and then began eating the last meal before Susan began her adventure.

Chapter 2

Susan followed the group of teenagers into the woods where they had prepared a party. She'd heard about these parties before—many of them ended with police getting involved somehow. She knew that she didn't want to spend all of her time here drinking beer, but she felt an obligation to try it at least once.

She stood at the edge of the clearing in the woods and watched all of her friends drinking and laughing and dancing. She sipped her own cup timidly, but soon the liquid sent a warm feeling over her and ironically, although she was outside, she felt that she needed fresh air.

She walked out of the woods by herself, surprised that it was so light outside still. The trees were so large and shady that she almost felt it was night. She walked along the road until she noticed a small shelter with a bench. She sat down on the bench and looked at the images around her. The one on the side of the wall of the shelter was a map with different color lines and pinpoints. Behind her with images of faces wearing too much makeup and announcing some sort of special dates.

Just then, she noticed a large vehicle driving down the road. It slowed to stop right before her and two doors automatically opened for her. The man who sat behind the wheel looked at her and said, "Hey, are you coming on or not?" Susan looked around to see if he could possibly be talking to anyone else, but there wasn't anyone else around.

She nodded and climbed up the large black steps leading inside of the vehicle. The bus driver looked her up and down and sighed audibly before shutting the doors behind her.

"I'm assuming you don't have any money to pay for this, do you?" The driver asked. Susan shook her head no and he just shrugged his shoulders and told her to take a seat in the back.

She walked towards the back of the bus, but before she found a seat, the driver took off and Susan lost her footing and fell into the seat where a young girl was sitting.

"Hey, watch out!" the girl shouted.

"I am so sorry," Susan apologized, "I wasn't prepared for the bus to move like that." The girl looked Susan up and down, obviously wondering about her long dress and bonnet. Instead of laughing at her or ignoring her, the girl smiled and patted the seat next to hers.

"Sit here," the girl said. She reached out her hand to Susan and introduced herself, "I'm Becky."

"It's wonderful to meet you, Becky," Susan smiled at her new friend, "I'm Susan."

"Cool," Becky said, "Where are you going?"

"Going?"

"Yeah, like, what stop are you getting off at?"

"I, uh, I'm not really sure exactly."

Becky looked at Susan and offered her a small rectangular device that lit up whenever she moved it.

"What is this?"

"Are you—what in the, where are you from? That's a cell phone. I thought you should probably call your parents or something and tell them that you're hanging out with me today!"

"Oh, that's very thoughtful. My mother knows I will be out for a while."

"Sounds good to me!" Becky clapped her hands together, "So, I was going to head to the mall. Do you want to come with me?"

"What's a mall?" Susan asked.

Becky smiled and responded, "Just stick with me, girl, and everything will be just fine."

Susan and Becky chatted with each other for the remainder of the bus ride with such ease, as if they had been long time friends. Susan told Becky about her life living in an Amish community and she explained the tradition of Rumspringa, which is why she was out experiencing the world.

"That is totally cool," Becky gushed, "I always thought that, like, you guys didn't really get a choice or anything."

"Not at all," Susan explained, "See we can't even get officially baptized in the church until we make the decision to do that. That's why we have this tradition so we can see how life is elsewhere and decide ultimately how we want to live."

"Do you know what you're going to decide?" Becky asked, but before Susan could respond, Becky yelled, "We're here! This is our stop. Come on!"

Susan climbed off the bus behind Becky and she stood on a busy street which faced a large glass building. The two girls made their way across the street and Susan found herself in a store surrounded by clothes—every style and color imaginable. She could not even fathom the idea of wearing some of things that she saw on the fake humans (mannequins, she heard Becky call them).

Becky grabbed a handful of different tops and jeans to try on and then headed to the back of the store where there was a fitting room. She put on each combination and then came out and paraded it around for Susan to judge whether or not she liked it. Of course, Susan didn't have much of an opinion on this type of fashion, so she would always say it looked great.

"Last one, Susan. What do you think?"

"Wow, Becky! I think that looks great!"

"It does, right?" Becky laughed, "Hey, I have an idea, you should totally try something on!"

Susan laughed, "No, I couldn't do that."

"Come on, come on, it will be fun. I promise!" Susan bit her lower lip debating whether or not she should try anything on. She felt like her mother would probably frown upon it, but at the same time, wasn't this the whole idea behind Rumspringa?

"Okay, I'll try on one thing," Susan decided. Becky clapped her hands in delight and handed her a pair of jeans that she had just tried herself. Susan went into the small room and closed the door behind her. She saw her reflection in the mirror as she undressed and she felt embarrassed by her own body. She quickly pulled her dress back on and slipped the jeans on under. Susan walked out of the room to show Becky.

"So?" Susan asked.

"Where are they?" Becky asked. Susan lifted the skirt of her dress slightly. "Wow, they look so good on you, Susan. You have to get them."

"I couldn't," Susan said feeling her cheeks getting hot.

"Let's go!" Becky said rushing them over to a small counter. She pushed all of her items towards a young woman standing on the other side.

"Will this be all?" the woman asked.

"Those too," Becky said pointing at the jeans Susan was wearing. She looked over at Susan with a huge smile on her face.

"Thank you, Becky. That is really very kind of you." Becky winked at Susan before handing over a small plastic card to take care of the transaction. Once Becky's items were folded into a small plastic bag, the two girls headed into the other side of the mall.

They walked side by side and Susan couldn't help but gawk at everything around her. The building was full of different stores selling so many things—clothes, electronics, furniture, baby things—she was starting to feel a bit overwhelmed by it all.

"And this," Becky said, stopping in front of a small booth with a curtain hanging over one side, "This is the real reason why I come to the mall."

"What is it?" Susan asked her.

"It's a machine that records you," Becky explained, "So it's like you sing karaoke, but it actually records you and makes an mp3 that you can take home!"

Susan just stared at her not even knowing where to begin with her questions.

"What?" Becky asked, noticeably disappointed in Susan's lack of a reaction, "You don't like singing?"

"Singing?" Susan repeated, "Oh, I sing every day with the choir. I love it! I just—well, I'm not sure, what is karaoke? And what is an mp3?"

Becky just laughed, "I'll show you. Let's go!" The two girls stepped inside of the machine and Susan watched as Becky inserted some money. The screen lit up and Becky scrolled through an endless list of song options. Finally, she selected an option and handed Susan a thing called a microphone. When Susan spoke into it, her voice was so much louder and she looked at Becky who just smiled.

The song started and it had a quick tempo. Susan watched words appear on the screen and suddenly, Becky started singing. Susan noticed that she sang whatever word came up and soon, Susan found herself nodding in time with the music. All too soon, the song ended and another screen popped up. Becky typed in something—she called it an email address—and explained that when she got home, she would be able to download the song and listen to it again.

Becky asked Susan if she wanted to try it, but Susan had no idea what any of these songs were, so she just shook her head. Becky did one more song and Susan wished that she was able to join in.

As the girls headed out from the mall, they waited at the bus stop together. Becky explained that they had to get on different buses now since Becky was heading home.

"Do you want to meet again tomorrow?" Becky asked, "We can try to do more songs!"

"Sure," Susan smiled, secretly wishing she could sing as well.

"Here," Becky said, handing her a small silver device. "This is called an iPod and it plays music. You just click this center button here, and put these in your ears, and the songs will play. Listen through them and tomorrow you can try one of these songs!"

Susan's eyes filled with small tears. She had known selflessness in her community, but for some reason, this kindness coming from this girl whom she just met struck her as being something amazing.

"Thank you, so much," Susan said. She boarded the next bus and waved at Becky as it pulled away from the bus stop. Following Becky's instructions, she rode the bus for about an hour before her stop. Once she got there, she walked the rest of the way back to the community.

She hid the iPod in her bonnet and made sure that her dress covered her new jeans completely. She couldn't believe that in one day, she experienced so much of the new world already.

She could only imagine how much more there was to learn.

Susan walked over to the side of the river and sat down beneath a shady tree. She pulled out the iPod and stuck the small white circles into her ears. Pressing the button, her ears were suddenly filled with the sounds of music. She sat there for a while, just listening as the various beats, melodies, and lyrics filled her head. Some songs Becky had even gave thanks to God, which made Susan smile.

Suddenly, she felt a tap on her shoulder. She jumped from her seat on the ground and ripped the earplugs out of her ear, struggling to hide it.

"Don't worry," the boy smiled, "I won't tell anyone."

Susan smiled appreciatively, "Thank you, Jacob." She tucked the iPod back under her bonnet and said, "It's Rumspringa. I met a nice girl and she let me borrow this device to listen to some songs."

"Do you like it?"

"Which? Rumspringa?"

"No, the music," he amended.

"Oh, yes," Susan gushed, "It really is quite catchy. But I do love the slower songs, some of the lyrics are beautiful."

Jacob nodded, understanding, "Yes, I remember. The music was one of my favorite parts of Rumspringa as well.

Can I tell you a secret?" Susan nodded. "I even though about leaving the community to try learning the drums!" Susan let out a quiet laugh.

"Oh, Jacob, you would never leave us," she said.

"No, I suppose that's why I ended up choosing the church after all," he smiled. "Can I walk you back home?" Susan nodded and the two of them walked together back to her house where her mother was waiting.

"So, have you thought about your decision? Do you know what you want to do yet?" Jacob asked.

"I think so," Susan said, smiling before walking up to the door of her house.

Jacob waved a final goodbye and walked away from the house as Susan pulled open the door and walked inside.

"Mother?" Susan called out, "Mother, I'm home!" She didn't hear a sound. Looking around the house, she finally found her mother curled up in her bed, asleep.

"Are you okay?" Susan rushed over to the side of her mother's bed and put the back of her hand to her mother's forehead.

Her mother mumbled something under her breath before pushing Susan's hand from her head.

"What did you say, mom? Are you feeling well?"

"I said," her mother was barely whispering and Susan had to lean forward to catch the rest of her words, "Please leave me alone."

Susan sat back on her heels. She debated her mother's words but she had never disobeyed her before. She left the room and pulled the door closed behind her. Susan could not even think of a time she ever saw her mother in bed before sundown, but she thought that perhaps she just wasn't feeling well and needed rest.

Susan went into her own room and pulled out the iPod again. She pushed in the ear plugs and pressed play, falling asleep to the new sounds washing over her.

Chapter 3

Susan woke up in the morning to loud clattering sounds coming from the kitchen. She got out of bed and pulled on her newly purchased jeans and pulled her dress over the top. She placed the iPod on top of her head and tied her bonnet securely in place, ensuring that nothing looked out of the ordinary.

She made her way into the kitchen to find her mother sitting at the table with her head in her hands.

"Mom?" Susan asked quietly. Her mother looked at Susan with a tear stained face. Her eyes were puffy and red. "Mom, what's wrong?"

Her mother shrugged her shoulders and smiled saying, "Nothing is wrong," she laughed, "I have no idea why I am crying. Just ignore me, Susie bug, I'm just a little out of it I suppose. Many things happening around here and you going on Rumspringa, I guess it's just hitting me."

"Do you want me to stay home today?" Susan asked.

"Don't be silly, Susan, of course that's not what I want. Go, go. Have fun!"

Susan smiled uncertainly at her mother but she stood from her seat anyways and headed towards the front door. Something was definitely going on with her mother—Susan could not even recall any time she'd ever seen her mother cry before. And she'd sent Susan out of the house without breakfast which she was certain had never happened in her 16 years of living.

She decided to try and leave it behind her as she left the community and walked towards the bus stop. Susan thought back to the directions that Becky had given her yesterday and waited for that specific bus. After about a ten-minute wait, the bus pulled up and Susan climbed on board. Becky was in the middle seats and waved at Susan as soon as her head appeared.

"No money again today?" the bus driver said. Susan looked at him and shrugged an apology, "I'm sorry but unless you have the bus fare, I can't let you on."

Susan looked back at Becky and said, "I'm sorry, Becky. He won't let me on unless I have the fare!" Becky jumped out of her seat and ran to the front of the bus plopping a few coins into a tall silver machine.

The bus driver looked at Susan and said, "You have a nice friend."

Susan nodded and replied, "I know." The two girls ventured further back in the bus and took their seats.

"So, did you get to listen to any of the songs on there?" Becky asked.

Susan nodded, "I actually fell asleep listening to all of your music! I love how different every song is and some of the lyrics are just incredible."

"I know, right?" Becky gushed, "Music is seriously my life. Do you know which song you want to try on karaoke today?"

"Does it let you record your own songs?" Susan asked.

Becky frowned, "No, it has to be one of the karaoke choices that are available. That's the only bad thing about this machine."

"Oh," Susan looked disappointed, "Well, I can watch you again today!"

"Wait a minute," Becky said, pulling out her phone, "I think I have an idea." Becky dialed a number quickly into her phone and pressed the call button. The volume was loud enough that Susan could hear when the woman answered on the other end. "Mom? Are you still home?" The woman mumbled something. "Okay, that's fine. I'm actually headed back to the house now instead of the mall." The woman responded with something and then the call ended.

Susan looked at Becky, curious to hear what the idea was that she looked so excited about.

"You've never heard of YouTube, right?" Becky asked. Susan shook her head no. "Well, prepare yourself for what I like to call a music-ation." Becky pulled out her phone and her ear plugs and offered one to Susan. After clicking and typing, a new screen opened and Susan watched a little spinning circle. She looked at Becky curiously.

Suddenly, her ears were filled with music and Susan was actually seeing the person singing. She watched in amazement at the small screen, truly appreciating the majesty of modern technology.

"This is amazing," she whispered to Becky.

"I know!" Becky laughed, "So, I think we should totally do it. Let's start our own YouTube channel! I have a webcam on my laptop at home and we can record ourselves singing random songs. It will be awesome!"

Susan couldn't help but smile at Becky. She wasn't confident in Becky's idea of them showing up on the other end of the screen, but Becky was so enthusiastic, it was hard not to catch on.

The girls watched video after video and Susan never ceased to be amazed by the various types of music from the slow, lyrical songs to the upbeat ones with funky dances. They all had one thing in common—they made Susan feel more alive than she had ever felt in her entire life.

The bus pulled to a stop and Becky announced that it was time for them to disembark. They shuffled off of the bus together and headed down the street towards Becky's house. Susan looked around at all of the houses—some were huge and had towering trees standing in the front areas of the house while others were a bit smaller, but still too big to be practical in any sense.

Becky walked up the driveway to one of the large houses and pulled out keys from her purse.

"Welcome to my home," Becky said, pushing the door open for Susan. The first thing Susan noticed was that everything was completely white—the floors were white; the walls were white and the furniture (except for a few pillows and blankets) were white.

"It's so..." Susan trailed off.

"Boring?" Becky laughed, "I know. But trust me, my room could not be any more different if I tried." Becky led the way upstairs and Susan couldn't help but wonder in the back of her mind what people do with all of this space.

Becky pulled open a door and Susan almost went into shock by the burst of color. Her walls were painted half hot pink, half orange. Becky had posters of different bands hanging all over her room and she had a bright purple comforter spread messily across her bed.

"This is my sanctuary," Becky said. She walked over to her small white desk and took a silver square from it. Becky walked Susan through exactly what they would do and how it would post to the internet. "It's really simple! I'll go first."

Susan watched as Becky turned on the camera and gave a small introduction of herself before starting the music in the background and singing her song. Once she was done, she uploaded the video to her YouTube channel.

"See?" Becky said to Susan, "Easy peasy! Now you go."

"I don't think I can, Becky. Besides, they don't even have my music on here."

"That's okay! You can sing acapella."

Susan hesitated a moment longer before finally agreeing to record a video. Becky clicked the button and pointed at Susan to begin.

Susan closed her eyes and called to her mind the melody and the words that brought her peace on so many occasions. She opened her mouth and the beautiful music began pouring out. She sang to no one—she sang to everyone. Music breathed a new life into her and it made her feel as though nothing could be wrong in the world.

Once she was finished, she opened her eyes and saw Becky sitting there with tears in her eyes.

"That was...beautiful," Becky choked out, "I had no idea you could sing that well." Susan smiled, not entirely comfortable with the attention but also pleased that Becky had enjoyed the song she chose.

The girls worked on their channel for the rest of the day, taking small breaks only to chat about the differences between their lives. Susan was starting to understand exactly how some people chose the modern world over the community. There just seemed to be so much more going on outside of her small community walls.

When Susan saw the time, she figured she should be heading back now to check on her mother. Becky gave her the bus directions and Susan smiled and hugged her tightly.

The two girls agreed to meet in the same place tomorrow.

Susan rode back in the bus by herself, listening to more songs from Becky's iPod. When she got to her stop, she hid it beneath her bonnet and walked towards the community. She reached her house and walked in not sure what to expect.

"Mother?" Susan called out.

"You're home early!" her mother cried out, appearing in the kitchen.

"I thought you would say I arrived late?" Susan asked.

"Nonsense, Susan. It's Rumspringa, it only happens once in your life. Anyways, how was your day?" Susan studied her mother carefully struck by the buzzing energy that surrounded her which was so different from yesterday when Susan had found her mother lying in bed and this morning when her mother had been in tears at the kitchen table.

"I had a great day," Susan decided to brush off the strangeness, especially because her mother looked to be in high spirits now. "I have made a friend and her name is Becky and we talk a lot about music."

"That's wonderful, Susan," her mother smiled at her and then walked into the kitchen. Susan offered her assistance, but her mother shooed her away and told her to get herself cleaned up.

Once Susan had finished washing up, she walked back into the kitchen and saw that the table was covered with food.

"Mother? Why is there so much food? Are we expecting company?"

"Oh, yes dear. Didn't I tell you? Jacob asked to join us for dinner tonight." Susan looked over at the table, even for three people this was too much food and it seemed almost wasteful to have prepared so much, but she let it go. There was a knock at the door and Susan walked over to open it and found Jacob standing there.

"Hello, Susan," he smiled.

"Jacob, please come in."

"How was your day today? Did you learn anything new?" he asked her, a mischievous gleam in his eye.

Susan smiled. She was tempted to tell him all about her YouTube channel, but hesitated and decided not to. She wasn't sure how Jacob would react if he'd found out that she had advertised herself and her talents to the world.

"Wow," Jacob said as he sat down at the table, "What a feast!"

"Well, it's a special occasion I think, isn't it? Anyways, it's not often that we have guests over the house. So, let's give our thanks to the Lord for blessing us with such bounty and let's eat the wonderful meal He has prepared through my hands." Susan's mother smiled at them both as she bowed her head and led them in grace.

Once they had finished, they begin passing around the plates. Susan asked, "What did you mean it was a special occasion, mom?"

Susan's mother looked up at Jacob and Susan saw him clear his throat nervously. He laughed, "Well, I wasn't expecting this all to happen so soon, but Susan, I just wanted to let you know that I have really grown fond of you and I hope that you feel the same way. I would like to spend more time with you if that's okay with you?"

Susan nearly choked on her food. She hadn't been prepared for this at all, especially not in front of her mother. They were both looking at her now, expecting her to answer, and she had no idea what to say.

"I'm quite sure Susan will say yes," her mother smiled at Jacob who started shifting in his chair uncomfortably. "Right, Susan?"

Susan recovered herself enough to respond, "Jacob, I would love to spend more time with you, but this is Rumspringa and as my mother said to me, it only happens once in a lifetime and—" Susan was cut short by the clattering sound at the end of the table. Her mother had pushed her own plate to the floor and stood up, looking extremely upset.

"How could you do this to me, Susan?" her mother started crying, "How?" She walked away from the table and went into her bedroom, slamming the door closed behind her.

Jacob looked at Susan with his eyebrows raised.

"I'm so sorry, Jacob!" Susan apologized, "I do not want you to think that I don't enjoy your company and of course, I would like to spend more time with you, it's just that, right now—" Jacob cut Susan off when he lightly touched her hand.

"I understand, Susan," he smiled, "I'm not upset at all. I enjoyed my time during Rumspringa and I would not want to take you away from that at all."

"Thank you so much for understanding," Susan smiled, slightly embarrassed now.

"Is your mother okay?" he asked.

"I'm not sure, Jacob. She has been acting strangely over the past two days. I found her yesterday in her bed before the sun had gone down and this morning she was in tears. She seemed perfectly fine tonight until just now. I'm not sure what could be wrong."

"Maybe she is just worried because you are gone," Jacob suggested.

"Maybe," Susan shrugged. They finished their meal and Susan led Jacob outside. They wished each other a good night and Susan cleaned the kitchen, picking up her mother's plate from the floor. She opened the door to her mother's room and found her asleep in her bed.

Susan knew that something was wrong, but she had no idea what it could be.

Chapter 4

For the following weeks, the routine was always the same. Susan would get up and meet Becky at the bus stop. They would go to Becky's house and record videos and post them on their YouTube channel. The two girls would read through the comments that people would leave—the majority of them were compliments though some people did not have pleasant things to say at all.

Becky told Susan that during the summers, she stayed with her dad at the other end of town and that's why she would have to take the bus to get over to her mom's house since her dad didn't allow her to bring her laptop. Susan felt a little guilty about the laptop, but she also secretly loved having someone who was showing here all of the wonderful things in the world.

Soon, Becky would be back at her mother's house for when school starts again. Susan wasn't sure what she would do then, but Becky suggested that Susan could follow her throughout school and they could say that she was shadowing Becky.

Susan quickly agreed to this plan because not only did it mean she would be able to maintain her YouTube channel and her friendship with Becky, but it also gave her the opportunity to explore education beyond 8th grade which excited her.

The first day of school came and Susan took the bus to Becky's house with no trouble. She laughed as she recalled her first day on the bus when she had no idea what it was and now she had become an expert at public transportation. Susan knocked on Becky's door and Becky's mother answered.

"You must be Susan," her mother smiled at her, "Becky has told me so much about you. Come in!" Becky was finishing getting dressed and she took about another 5 minutes before she came downstairs.

"Susan!" Becky yelled excitedly, "You'll never believe what my mother bought me for my first day back to school!"

"What is it?" Susan asked, laughing at Becky's crazy eyes.

"A car! Come look, come look!" Becky led Susan out to the garage and opened the door and revealed a small, blue car with two doors. "It's not brand new or anything, but still. I'm so excited. We get to drive to school in style," Becky laughed, "Come on, let's go!"

The two girls rode together in the car with the music blasting. Susan felt amazing—as if nothing in the world could stop her. She loved feeling so free. The car ride ended too quickly as they pulled up in the parking lot for the school. Becky parked and the two of them got out of the car.

"Hey!" Becky and Susan turned around to see a boy with ashy brown hair waving at them.

"Hi Robert," Becky smiled as the boy walked up to them.

"Nice wheels!" he gushed when he saw Becky's car.

"Thanks!" Becky shook her keys excitably. "This," she said directing her attention to Susan, "is my best friend Robert. Probably the coolest dude you'll ever meet."

"Hey," he said, extending his hand out to Susan, "It's really nice to finally meet you, Susan. I've watched all of your videos—you have got one stellar voice!"

Susan blushed as she shook his hand and said, "Thank you."

The three of them walked into the school together, Becky and Robert complaining about how much work they would have to do even though it was only the first day. Susan was almost overwhelmed by the number of students here—so many different types of people walking through the hallways, talking with their friends about what they did over the summer.

A peppy blonde girl walked up to them and said, "Hey guys! Did you already buy your tickets to the dance?"

Robert replied, "Come on, Penny. We haven't even gotten our schedules yet, let alone tickets to a dance."

"You have to go, Robert," the girl whose name was Penny smiled at him and brushed his arm gently, "It's the back to school dance."

Robert nodded and looked over at Susan, "The only way I'll go is if she goes with me."

"Me?" Susan asked, clearly not expecting that to come from his mouth. Robert nodded and smiled.

"Will you go with me to the dance?" Susan agreed to go with him and the three of them walked over to the table to purchase the tickets. Robert handed one ticket to Susan and told her, "Don't lose this." Susan saw Penny roll her eyes, obviously not pleased with how all of that played out.

The rest of the day went by in a blur and Susan was exhausted by the end. Becky asked if she wanted to come over, but Susan thought it would be better to go home and check on her mother.

The bus ride passed in a blur and Susan was back at the stop before she knew it. She got off and headed back to her community where Jacob was waiting.

"Hey Jacob. What's going on?"

Jacob looked a little upset, "Your mother isn't doing too well, it seems Susan. Today she started yelling at the other women and telling them all that they were being lazy and that the Lord was watching them."

Susan felt drained, but she knew she couldn't deny that her mother needed her. She walked home and found her mother already in her bed asleep. Jacob sat down with her on the front porch as Susan put her face in her hands.

"I can't leave her," Susan mumbled. She thought back to the day and how happy she'd felt. She thought about Robert and the way his hand had touched hers when he'd given her the dance ticket. She imagined dancing with him and a sad smile crossed her lips.

"What is it?" Jacob asked.

Susan looked at him and said, "As the days pass, I become more and more tempted to stay in the modern world. They have so much to offer, but with all of that comes a price. People lose their sense of real happiness because they start relying on material things to make them happy."

Jacob looked over at Susan and took her hand in his. He nodded at her to continue.

"I think I would be happy for a little while out there," Susan admitted, "But after a while, I would be searching for something else, never even realizing that all I ever needed was home."

"Are you saying what I think you are saying?" Jacob asked.

Susan looked up at him and smiled, "I'm saying that I am staying here."

# THEIR AMISH LOVE

## ALICE EVANS

<u>Prologue:</u>

The tears begin to pool at Laura's feet as she rests her head in her hands. Propped up against the window frame, she begged for the pain to stop as she watched the world around her turn. They couldn't see. They wouldn't care enough to try. As the day drug on, one more piece of her shattered existence faded away as their smiles and laughter filled the outreaches of her mind. As their days rolled on, all of the things she had so desperately pushed down into the back of her mind had begun to rip her soul to shreds. Nothing in her life had ever been easy, but she never once complained; that wasn't who she was. Laura Miller stood in the face of adversity and simply stated that God had a plan for her and if this adversary is what He intended for her, she was willing to stand her ground with Him by her side.

For the first time in thirty-five years of living, however, she couldn't. For the first time, she couldn't hold onto the singular force in her life. Because if she aligns herself with Him, then she must also agree to the terms that the same person who is on her side is the same person on... *his*. After giving him ten years... ten years of devotion, love, and care, she must remain silent. Her cries muffled, her pain ignored. Then all at once, the pain becomes too much and as she clutches her chest, Laura falls to her knees; knocking into the bookcase.

As the Good Book falls beside her, her vision clears just long enough to read one verse; Isaiah 64:8. *"Yet you, LORD, are our father. We are the clay, you are the potter; we are all the work of your hand."* Whether fate, need, or celestial intervention, Laura dries her face and uses the limits of her strength to rise to her feet. She knows that whatever she chooses to do next, it will change everything. There is nothing she can do, but she can no longer sit around in passive silence. She must confront her fear and remain unshaken in her faith... but as she turns, her mind flings back once more to before this all began.

*"how did I end up here..."*

<u>Chapter One</u>

You are one in a million; there never has been or will there ever be someone who is exactly like you. Laura Miller heard this phrase uttered by every mother after she helped them to deliver their child. Hearing those few words always sparked a great warmth that would wash over her and spread throughout the home being created. This thought, of course, was always followed by a murmured chuckle as Laura realized how juvenile she was being. Despite these thoughts entering her mind, she had decided many years previous that she could not be happy without her job as a midwife. From the newborn coos to the mother's tears the moment she gets to hold her child for the first time, Laura found that nothing else in this Earth bound life could ever bring her the same joy.

For this, she considered herself very lucky. Some people are not as fortunate as she was in finding that her work and her passion in life were aligned completely. Whether due to financial constraints, personal inability, or and other number of factors, not everyone is afforded the same luxuries she praised God for everyday. As she packed up her kit to go into town, the hired hand her husband had hired to help fix the roof knocked on the door jam before entering.

"Ms. Miller, there's someone here to see you, ma'am."

"Thank you, Jeremiah, you can send them in." Jeremiah nodded his head and moved aside for a woman to enter her home.

"Thank you, ma'am for welcoming me into your home. I am sure you are quite busy so I won't take up much of your time-"

"Slow down, child. My schedule should not concern you. Besides, unless the Lord has any plans for Susan Price's child to be born two months early, my schedule is all but cleared for the day." The small woman stood in front of her, and though she smiled, her body language betrayed her true feelings. Short in stature, and thin in frame, if her cheeks hadn't been so flushed, Laura would have been convinced that she was sickly or malnourished. Scanning over the woman's stance and overall demeanor, Laura could tell that something wasn't quite right with the picture she was seeing.

"Would you care to sit?" Laura floated her hand to usher the woman into her kitchen. It took the woman a minute to collect herself as she situated herself in Laura's grandfather's handmade chairs. "What's your name, dear?"

"Sarah. Sarah Fisher."

"Oh, you are Ihrm and Mary Fisher's daughter right?" Sarah nodded her head briskly. "I don't think I've ever had the pleasure of meeting you. Though, somehow I feel like you already know me."

"Please don't think me intrusive. Susan is a friend of mine and she told me that you were the best person in town to speak to about... well really anything." At this point, Sarah's words flew from her lips. As if she had been bottling up her words for far too long.

"Susan speaks too highly of me. Maybe you would be better speaking to Preacher King. He lives just up the road if you would like me to escort-"

"NO!" The strength and anguish in her voice startled Laura; and frankly would have sent her reeling if she had been standing. Noticing the confusion her exaltation had invoked, Sarah quickly searched to find the words to save face. "What... What I mean to say is.... Well..."

"You want to talk to a woman, not a man is what I am gathering. Is that right?" Sarah nods her head vigorously.

"It's not that I feel shameful or like I am doing something wrong that the preacher can help me with.... I feel I just needed to talk to someone like you; especially after hearing about how helpful you have been for Susan throughout her pregnancy." Laura watched as Sarah's hand left her lap and began cradling her stomach. Though it had gone unnoticed before, Laura could now see a distinguishable outline.

"Sarah, are you pregnant?"

"Yes. Or at least, I think I am. My husband says we are so lucky to be blessed so soon after our wedding, and I agree..."

"But?"

"But... I wish I had been given more time to prepare for this. What if I mess something up and end up hurting my child?"

"The fact that that is your biggest concern proves to me that you will do nothing of the sort. Believe me, I have sat with many an expectant mother and they all share the same fears brewing in your mind. You fear that the love you have won't be enough; you worry that your husband won't care for you the same after the baby comes; you fear that you will somehow mislead the child and that he won't follow in our ways; I have heard every fear and worry in the book."

"And what do you tell them?"

"I tell them that it is all going to be alright. The Lord does not give His people something that they cannot handle; but that doesn't mean that it is sinful or shameful to ask for help. We all have good and bad days, but being honest about that makes it easier to make it to the other side." Sarah's face began to brighten as Laura's words of encouragement and love began to sink in.

"Thank you, Miss."

"You may call me Laura if you like." Sarah's smile then widened to encapture her whole face and the color had begun to return to her skin.

"Thank you Laura."

<u>Chapter Two</u>

"That's Mrs. Miller to you, girl." A gruff voice filled the house as Laura gripped the cloth in her skirt.

"Ephraim, please."

"I'd keep my mouth shut if I were you, Laura." Laura pushed her energy into her feet to stand, but she couldn't make herself move.

"I'm not sure who you are and I will apologize if I frightened you. However, I need to speak with my *wife* and I am going to ask you only once to leave my house." Sarah's eyes darted between the scene unfolding before her eyes. She nodded her head once before quickly exiting. Laura wished to have the courage to express herself before

Sarah's shadow escaped the stoop, but her eyes blazed with fear as her husband walked over to her.

A statuesque man, Laura always considered herself to be quick lucky to "land him." Before her father died, he insisted that he see Laura be married to a God-fearing, stand-up man who could take care of her. From the moment they were introduced, Laura was inexplicably smitten. From his dark auburn hair to his piercing green eyes with the little blue flecks, not only was he a man of God, but he was the kind of man she always imagined herself with. Less than three months after their courtship began they were married. The wedding was a large affair, larger than any other the town had experienced and they were gilded with praise and admiration for being the most successful match the community had ever seen.

But what happened behind closed doors was different. The first few months, even years were fine. They were happy and nothing seemed remiss. But as they approached their fifth wedding anniversary, something in him changed. As much love and support that Laura would afford her husband, he stopped smiling. The person the town saw during the day was not the man she would come home to at night. The man she knew and believed to be kind, open and charitable turned mean-spirited, harsh and oftentimes rude. Laura, despite all of this, gave him the benefit of the doubt. Maybe the business isn't doing well, maybe he isn't feeling good; perhaps he's just having a bad day... all these things and more ran through her head as she created excuse after excuse for his differing behavior towards her and others. This continued for another five years and unbeknownst to her, their tenth anniversary was about to pass them by.

Laura's inner monologue of running through the changes in her husband's behavior became readily apparent to him as he threw his hat down.

"What are you thinking about? What?"

"Ephriam, are you alright?"

"What, you work as a midwife and you fancy yourself a doctor?"

"That's not what I meant," Laura's mood began to fall as her husband's harsh expression fell on her heart. "I'm just worried about you. I am your wife, you should be able to confide in me about everything, and if something is going on that I need to know about-"

"Why would I talk about anything of any importance with you when you are never around?"

"I don't understand..."

"What, you have time for every terrified girl bringing new life into this world, but you can't afford me anytime at all?"

"When have I ever prioritized my work over my love for you?"

"When haven't you?"

"Ephraim, please, you aren't making any sense. What do you want from me?"

"Why? Am I scaring you?" Laura, now stood across the room, had laced her fingers around the locket encircling her neck. Her eyes unable to flutter from his. As piercing and afraid his expression made her, she could never seem to remove her gaze. As much and as often he confused her and conjured up fear in her heart, her love for him was unyielding.

"What, you can't find the words?"

"I don't know what you want me to say. I have sat beside you day after day as you changed before my eyes. My love for you has never faltered and even now with these accusations all I ask is that you are honest with me about what you want. Something has been bothering you for so long, but you won't talk to me." Laura could feel her own voice increasing in intensity. "Just tell me what you want! I can't read your mind!" Angry tears flow down her cheeks as she can no longer hide how unhappy she had become.

Ephraim felt every tear as if it were his own as they rained down his wife's cheeks. He knew what he was doing hurt her, but something in him was telling him that it was for the best. The hurt she felt now is what she deserved for taking him for granted all of these years.

"You want to know what I want?" Laura's eyes close as more tears stream down her face and shakes her head; as if begging him to reveal his pain to her. As he stares at her, looking for any shred of sincerity, he states his desires through the use of one word.

"Quit." And with that, Laura's heart broke.

Chapter Three

They didn't speak the rest of the night. Laura's heart hung heavy in her chest as she laid herself to bed that night. She didn't realize how unhappy her work had made him. But as these thoughts plague her mind, she feels Ephraim lay down beside her. Every bone in her body wants to roll over and wrap her arms around him; to provide him some sort of comfort that he can't seem to find within himself. As she shifts her weight in the bed, she feels him turn away from her, as if knowing the desires in her heart. Muffling her tears, she closed her eyes and drifted off.

Laura often found solace in her dreams, believing that God would often speak to her through her dreams and help to guide her towards finding the answers she needed. She prayed before finally drifting off to sleep for Him to give her a sign or to help her understand her husband's sudden fury with her desire to continue working. Tonight, however, it was not an abstract, objective vision but a walk through her own memories. She flies through her inner timeline until everything stops and she lands in a memory from so many years ago she had nearly forgotten about it's passing...

*"Are you enjoying yourself, Laura?"* Laura watches on as her younger self walked through the meadow with the younger version of the man she loved inquired of her feelings.

*"This is lovely Ephraim. How did you manage to find this place?"*

*"Well while everyone else went out on Rumspringa I stayed behind to help my father and mother in their shop. They are going to hand it over to*

*me one day, you know and I thought then was as good a time as any to get started learning the business."*

*"I'm sure they greatly appreciated that. But didn't you ever regret not getting to go out and experience the world before beginning your life?"* Laura, watching on, did not take that much stock into his responses or expressions that day, but she now finds herself unable to look anywhere else. She hid behind the seemingly singular tree in the vast valley she found herself remembering; though she chastised herself for hiding because as this is just a memory why should she be hidden? She, after all, was the one who needed to figure out why God was showing this to her.

*"Why would I leave when I have everything I could possibly need right here? Besides, now that you are back, why would I ever need to leave?"* Both Laura's blush uncontrollably.

"Ephraim, please."

"What? Do you know how distressed I was when you left?"

"We had never met before our fathers introduced a few months ago."

"No, but I saw you when you left town that day."

"You did?"

"As I saw you with your suitcase in tow begin to walk away from town, I ran up to the roof of my parent's shop to get a better look at you. From the instant I laid eyes on you I thought you were the most beautiful girl I had ever seen."

"Ephraim-"

"I didn't know how long you were going to be gone, but I knew that I would wait as long as it took for you to return."

"But you didn't know me. I could have been deranged or incompatible... what made you do a silly thing like that?" Ephraim stopped in his tracks, turning back to face her. Plucking a bright yellow field from her feet, he places it behind her ear; caressing her face as his hand falls to lock with hers.

"Something in me just knew. Whether that was God or my heart, I believe that He wanted me to know to wait for you to return. I mean I didn't think it would take four years, but better late than never I guess." Laura lightly wacks Ephraim with her free hand as he pulls her with him, running through the meadow.

Laura awoke as she felt herself intertwine with her past self as she was pulled into the meadow by the man snoring loudly beside her. Rubbing the vision from her eyes, the room was pitch black. She had no new answers, just further confusion.

"Why that memory?" She pondered aloud.

"Go back to sleep, Laura."

"Ephraim! I'm sorry, did I wake you?"

"Just because I'm angry doesn't mean I am not still concerned when my wife wakes up in the middle of the night for no discernable reason." Laura feels a smile and a small spark light in her chest. "Go to sleep, Laura."

She reaches to place a hand on her husband's shoulder, but finds herself holding herself back. She found herself at a disadvantage to her husband. Though she had never questioned his love for her, she never knew the depth of his love for her. That memory from so long ago that was tossed aside because of a frivolous girl's temperament now broke this woman's heart. A man who loved her so much to wait for her to return to their world couldn't answer for why she stayed away for so long. As much as she wanted to, everything they had built together would be destroyed if she did. Letting loose a sigh, her head falls back towards her pillow and she closes her eyes trying to escape the guilt boiling in her gut.

<u>Chapter Four</u>

When she woke up in the morning, Ephraim was nowhere to be found. She ventured around the house and both the front and the back yard before re-entering the kitchen. As she runs her fingers absentmindedly over the splits in the wooden table, she yelped as her fingers brush a piece of paper, slicing her fingers. As she tended to her fingers, she looked down to find a crumpled piece of paper lying on the table. Laura felt a stone lodge in her heart as she flattened out the piece of paper to read its inscription:

Laura,

I will be home tonight at five, at which point we need to discuss your leaving your work to come stay at home and take care of things around the house. Please be home on the time I have spoken or else we will be discussing other matters with Preacher King.

Yours.

It was hard for Laura not to crack a smile at the way he signed the note. As heartwrenching a message, his signature took her back to before they were married and he signed all his letters - not with his name or a funny anecdote, but with one small little word to prove to her that he was hers utterly. Because of his signature still finding its way onto this note, she clings to the hope that they will overcome the situation they are facing together. However... that also means she will have to tell her husband the truth.

At this exact moment of pivotal decision making, Laura is startled by a knock on the door, followed by a loving voice.

"Laura? It's Susan. I've brought Sarah with me, are you home?" Laura crossed the room to the door.

"Hello Susan, Sarah. Would you like to come in?" As the women enter into Laura's home, it is clear they notice something is off about Laura.

"Are you sure? I mean, we can come back once you've changed and fixed yourself..." Laura immediately takes her hand to her head and feels the tousled mess her hair had become. Embarrassed, she asked the woman to wait in the kitchen while she quickly through on a new outfit and wrangled her hair into a bun tucked neatly at the nape of her neck.

When she reemerged, the woman seem relieved that she has returned to her normal state.

"What brought you to my doorstep this morning? Is it labor pains? I promise it's probably just a false alarm. I've yet to be wrong about false labor."

"No, no, nothing like that. Sarah came to see me yesterday after leaving here yesterday and I wanted to come and check in to make sure that everything is alright because clearly something is going on and to be honest we are worried." Words fell from Susan's lips, quicker and more abrasive than she meant them.

"What Susan means is, are you and Ephraim okay? It just seemed so out of character for the behavior I saw yesterday..."

"We just want to know that you are okay and we want you to know that you can talk to either of us whenever you need to about anything. You have done so much for the women of this town that it seems only right that we pay it forward in their stead." Laura felt both a wave of acceptance and terror at their words of encouragement. After fifteen years of keeping her secret, could anyone forgive her? Her breaths catch in her throat as she attempts to decide whether or not she will allow them in or continue hiding her grief from more people who care about her. As she took one long inhale and exhale, she lets her gaze linger between the two women.

"What I say here does not leave here." The women sit to the front of their chairs, leaning in to see what could possibly have the strong woman they know and love so scared. "Susan, you knew me before I went away."

"We were in school together and you introduced me to my husband. I'm forever grateful you brought him into my life."

"Well, yes. But after I came back from my Rumspringa, you were the first person I went to see." Laura paused to gather thoughts. "You didn't question why I had been gone so long, you didn't tell me how much you missed me, and you didn't ask fifty questions all at once;

because the one question you did ask was enough." Susan gathered her memories in her mind to find what Laura was referring to.

"I... I asked you what happened because you looked awful. We thought that the family you had stayed with had hurt you in some way. I never really believed you when you said that they were nothing but kind to you. How could they have been when you came back looking like that?"

"What did you look like?" A perfectly innocuous question, fell on the harsh expression of Susan; letting Sarah know that it may not have been the place for that line of questioning.

"It's alright Sarah; Susan, you remember better than I do surely." Susan, annoyed at Laura's demand for her to recount a time in her life she would rather forget.

"She looked half-dead. From the bruising around her eyes, the pale white her hair had turned, the sheer loss of body weight... we were convinced you had been tortured or worse."

"In a way, I was... but not in the way you are thinking."

<u>Chapter Five</u>

Sarah and Susan stare intently at their confidant as she searches for the right way to express herself.

"Okay... so I am going to walk you through what happened to me, and I need you to just sit and listen. Please no interjections or I am not sure I will be able to make it through this." The women nod their heads in solidarity. Laura shuts her eyes and enters into her past.

*It was the third month I was in New York City. The family I was staying with took me to Times Square, this big plaza full of tourists and so many different kinds of people. It was beautiful. We went and saw a Broadway show and on our way home, I began to feel a bit off. I had been getting tired a lot recently and the pain in my stomach wasn't new either. Though I all but actually drug my heels into the ground, they took me to the hospital. After doing some tests, a tall, brooding man in a white coat came to the side of my bed. He looked stern - but that is how everyone in that world looked. I will never forget what he told me.*

*"Miss. I'm not quite sure how to tell you this, but you have end stage ovarian cancer." Though I didn't know what his words meant, I knew that it was something incredibly serious.*

*"Basically, the cancerous cells have formed cysts on your ovaries causing you the abdominal pain and the feeling of exhaustion from your body trying to fight the diseased cells. It is rare for someone of your age to have this aggressive of a strain unless you were predisposed to this condition genetically. Now, this is going to sound indelicate, however, did either your mother or grandmother have any issues like this?"*

"Did they?"

"Sarah! What did she say about interruptions?" Laura let out a wry laugh as they squabbled. When they looked up at her, Susan gestured for her to continue.

*"My mother died when I was born, and I never met my grandmother." The doctor proceeded to look at my chart, wringing his head.*

*"We need to get you booked into an ER immediately to do an emergency hysterectomy. You won't live more than six months without the operation."*

*"Don't worry Laura, we are taking care of everything. We will take care of any expense to make sure you can go back home healthier than you left."*

*"Wait... wait... what is a hysterectomy?"*

*"Well... again, I am sorry about how this sounds, but we need to go in and remove your ovarian tract because - if you want to look at your scans - there is no hope for saving them and the cancer is already beginning to spread. Unfortunately, as this procedure is highly invasive, you will have to undergo serious treatment and the recovery period could be anywhere from six months to two years." Laura's heart fell to her feet. She couldn't believe what she was being told.*

*"Okay. Well what are the long term effects of this procedure? Like, if I get it I can live a normal, healthy life?"*

*"Completely. The only thing that will be adversely affected will be that you will not be able to conceive naturally."*

"Wait a minute... you - you can't have children?" Susan's frame has shifted from the front of her chair to the back; as if all the wind had been knocked out of her.

"I fought getting the procedure... but I wasn't getting any better. And the thought of my father being here all alone, I knew I had to get better to come home to him."

"Oh my word."

"The procedure took a lot out of me, and I had to be put into this coma thing so that my body could begin to heal itself. I woke up almost eight months later; healed, but heartbroken."

"Why have you kept this from everyone? I mean, you almost died... Wait," Sarah's brain catches up with her words, "does Ephraim know?"

"No... but I feel I am going to have to tell him soon. He wants me to quit being a midwife."

"What! NO! I need you and Sarah is going to need you as her pregnancy progresses. You are the best midwife in the whole county."

"Susan, did you ever wonder why I wanted to be a midwife?"

"I just assumed that people in your family had or you just liked helping people."

"Though I do enjoy helping people on one of the most pivotal and important moments in their lives, there is a far more selfish reason I work so hard and so long with all of you. It's because when I help women deliver their babies, I am able to - just for a split second - experience the same euphoria they do and I feel less broken."

"But you aren't broken, Laura..." Sarah reaches out a hand to comfort her friend but Laura bats it away as her hot, angry tears boil over onto her cheeks.

"How would you know? Both of you have children growing in your stomachs and- and I can't have children."

"The Lord must've had a larger plan for this. I mean, you may not be able to have children, but ask any woman you have helped and they will tell you that if you hadn't been there they wouldn't be sure that they would have been able to make it through in one piece." Sarah and Susan began to cry with Laura.

"I-I just don't know how I am going to be able to tell Ephraim. I know I have to, that has become clear."

"How do you think he will react?" Susan inquires as she places her hands on Laura's.

"Why don't you turn around and ask him yourself?"

<u>Chapter Six</u>

Ephraim's gruff voice catches in his throat. Laura's eyes go wide, unable to look behind her to where his voice came from. Sarah and Susan look up to meet Ephraim's gaze, before they look back down at the terrified Laura.

"We are going to leave you two to talk." Susan stands up and grabs Sarah's wrist to guide her to the door. Sarah stalls for a second to hug Laura and only released as she whispered in her ear,

"Take a deep breath and just tell him. It will be okay." Sarah smiles as she is drug away by Susan, leaving Ephraim slouched against the door frame as Laura shrunk back into her seat. Nothing was said and no one moved for what felt like eons. Finally, because otherwise she felt she was going to go mad, Laura raised her tear stained face to ask,

"How much did you hear?"

"Every word."

"I thought you weren't going to be back until tonight."

"I... I left... well now I can't remember what I left, are we really not going to address what I just heard?"

"Look, we were fine before when you didn't know and we can be fine again. Just pretend you don't know anything and then I can go back to compartmentalizing the guilt I feel and you can go back to being angry with me or whatever you want. Just please... please pretend this didn't happen this way."

"Would you ever have told me if I didn't find out this way?" The silence between them was deafening as Laura decides that she can no longer go on lying.

"No. I wasn't. After this long, too much time had passed. And after your behavior shift a few years ago I couldn't risk you using this knowledge about me as ammunition against me to nullify our union. Because for whatever reason you are mad at me, there has not been on second, one moment since we met that I have not been completely and wholeheartedly in love with you."

"I am such a fool." Laura's sobs catch in her throat as she feels her husband approach her back and squat down in front of her to meet her gaze. "All this time I thought you were working as a midwife because you didn't want your own kids, while the whole time you have been keeping this secret from me because you were scared I would leave you? How poor a husband am I that I led you to believe that you couldn't rely on me absolutely in every aspect of your life?" Laura broke down into heart wrenching, gut punching sobs as she throws her arms around her husband. His hands pushing her closer to him, holding her tighter than he ever had before.

"I - I just couldn't live with the thought of you hating me for deceiving you for all of these years. It wasn't that I didn't want to stay home and be a housewife, it was that I couldn't stay home and be a housewife because I lack the ability to do the one thing housewives are supposed to give their husbands: children..." Laura stopped a moment to breathe, "I... I can't give you children."

"Why didn't you just talk to me about this?"

"Because I am ashamed. If not only for the fact that I accepted outside medical care, I became ashamed of my secret and it felt as if too much time had passed and I had missed my opportunity." Ephraim pulls back for a moment, taking his hand and wiping away her tears.

"I never want to hear you tell me that you are ashamed of yourself ever again. If anyone should be ashamed it is me. I didn't trust in your love for me and I didn't discuss my issues with our circumstances openly with you. I went and stewed behind your back only causing more anxiety for you and breaking our relationship even further."

"But my lies are what started it all. I am so sorry Ephraim, can you ever forgive me?"

"Laura, you are the woman I love, have always loved, and will always love. As angry and bitter as I had become, this was the last possible thing I could have conjured up to have been the reason for your neglectance to want to stay in the home."

"I love you too." Laura's sheepish confession caused Ephraim to cradle her chin in his hands, trying to find his eyes in hers. When she did finally meet his gaze, she saw something so wonderful, she thought she would never stop crying: Ephraim was smiling.

<u>Epilogue</u>

It would take much time and counseling from the elders of the community, but soon after all was revealed, Laura and Ephraim were on the path to rebuild their life together. As strong as their relationship had been, without their revelations, Laura had been sure that they would have never lasted. It has been three years since Laura was able to tell her husband the truth; and in those three years, Laura and Ephraim's relationship became strong. To show his solidarity with her work, he built her an addition on their house. In which she counseled and provided assistance to young - and oftentimes frightened - mothers-to-be; she also used the space to teach other women the skills she had acquired so she could give him the gift he wanted: more time together.

Relationships have their ebbs and flows, but trust is the stone that can either break the walls or build the castle. After their trust in eachother had been utterly destroyed by misunderstanding, it took a long time to build each other back up; and they may never finish rebuilding... But by growing together, they found that they could do anything, just so long as they had the Lord in their hearts and each other in their eyes. For God gives us nothing that we can't handle, and if it becomes too hard, He gives us each other to find solace in.

# My Amish Roots

## Nicola Meyer

Chapter 1

Haylee lay in the darkness of her room staring out of the window at the moon that hung low in the sky, her only consort in her lonely life. Four years after meeting Jase, her heart was broken into a million pieces and scattered across the vast expanse of her own insignificant universe. Move on, they said, he's not worth it, they said, you deserve better. What did they know? None of her so called friends could ever imagine how she felt deep down and how utterly destroyed she was when she walked in on Jase in the arms of her best friend, Lucile. Of course the first thing both of them shouted when caught in the act was – it's not what you think!

After Jase pleaded with her and Lucile convinced her that it was an irresponsible judgement error on her part and that it would never happen again, she gave it another shot. She should have known better. Naïve little Haylee, who only tries to see the good in people ended up as the biggest fool of them all and when it happened a second time, she could no longer be ignorant. It was obvious that between the chemical combination of Lucile's raging pheromones and Jase's ego boosted testosterone, she never stood a chance. She had to finally admit to herself that she was never going to find true love, and friendships are feeble pastimes for pre-schoolers.

It's been almost two months since her relationship with Jase ended, and it wasn't long after that, that she also handed in her resignation as an article clerk. Breaking up with Jase and seeing him once in a blue moon she could handle well, but working with him and sharing the same open office day in and day out was a little too much to handle. It amazed her how men in could be so callous and move on without a worry in the world. She had managed thus far, but the more she sat at home she started to feel cooped up like a bird in a too small cage.

She sighed and tugged her blanket over her shoulders and tucked it under her chin as she turned onto her other side, this time staring at her graduation photo. She stood tall and proud, alone in her toga with her rolled up certificate in her hand, no immediate family to share her successes with her. Her adoptive mother had passed away six months short of her graduation that year. Haylee sniffed and blinked away the tears. She didn't cry then and she won't cry now. Finally giving up on sleeping she tossed the blanket back and sat up in bed. Her mom always told her, that every person has left something behind in their past, that sits there and waits until they go back to find it and resolve it. And until recently she had never thought she wanted to go back there. She was only four when she was adopted, a lonely gray mouse stuck in foster care. From the first day she arrived at her new family, she was accepted and spoiled rotten. She never needed for anything in her life, and she never felt as if she was any different to any of the other kids, so why she suddenly felt like digging out the past was a mystery to her, but every day it became more and more pressing. And here at two in the morning, she was stuck between forcing herself to sleep or logging into her email to see if the adoption agency managed to track down her biological mother or family. Insomnia won the battle and she finally made herself a cup of coffee and sat down at her desk and logged into her emails.

Dear Miss Jones

We have managed to track down your biological mother, but it is with regret that we inform you that she passed away a few years ago due to illness. We have however managed to track down her parents, your grandparents. We do however wish that you consider the fact that they may not...

Hayley stared at the email, reading it over and over again, somehow grief evaded her, and it was like reading the sad story of a stranger. What she did learn from this was that her mother was born Amish, and that her grandparents lived in an Amish community in Ethridge, Tennessee. But even if she knew who they were, what good would that do now? It wasn't as if she could reunite with her long lost mother anymore. But what she might be able to figure out is what type of woman her mother was and what type of life she lived. Maybe it will even shed some light on why her mother gave her up for adoption. As she spent her time reading up on the Amish and their culture, it became more and more evident that her mother may not have had a choice, but this was pure speculation. And unless she took the time to find these things out for herself, she would always be guessing about the woman who brought her into this world.

Besides, it wasn't as if she had anything better to do with her time. She had no job, no love life and no coffee, she thought as she looked at the empty canister in front of her.

That was it; she was going to take the last of her savings and head to Ethridge and find the Lapp's.

Chapter 2

The whole way to Ethridge, Hayley kept wondering if she was making a mistake. She was about to embark on a journey she was in the least bit prepared for. Before she left everything behind, she made effort to reinvent her wardrobe with a few modest outfits just so that she wouldn't look too outrageous amongst the Amish. But even now as she sat in the back of the cab, her heart was beating a million miles a second and she was on the verge of having a nervous breakdown. She had just left behind the only life she knew, not that there was much left of her for her to salvage, but she was somewhat comfortable where she was.

The cab pulled into the small town of Ethridge and stopped in front of what appeared to be a touring business.

"This is as far as I can go," the cab driver said and pointed to this meter.

Hayley nodded and fished for cash to pay the cab driver and the moment her bags were offloaded and she stood like a singled out deer in hunting season outside on the sidewalk she wanted to burst out in tears. Whatever was she thinking coming out here?

"Hello, may I help you?"

Startled Hayley nearly lost her balance as she spun to look at the stranger behind her, "Oh-I-um, well, I'm looking for someone," she said and dug in her purse, "Mr. and Mrs. Lapp?"

"Oh Fredrick and Mary Lapp, yah, they live here. I can take you," the young man said.

"You know them?" Hayley asked in disbelief.

"Yah, well it's a small community we all know each other," he said tucking his thumbs under his suspenders.

Hayley couldn't help but stare, wondering if all Amish men were this good looking. This guy couldn't be much older than her twenty-five. And although he was dressed modestly in what she had to assume Amish clothes, he looked reasonably attractive. He had ebony black hair with willow green eyes set deeply in his skull.

"If you're done staring..." he said interrupting her thoughts with his brows drawn together.

Embarrassingly she shook her head, "I'm so sorry, I just... it has been a really long day and I've traveled a long way."

"No matter, my name is Duncan," he said and nodded his head courteously, extending his hand.

"Hayley," she said and gave his hand an overly firm shake.

"Well I best be getting you to the Lapp's, the weather is turning foul."

Without notice he started loading her luggage into a carriage that stood nearby and then patted the back of the carriage, indicating her seat.

Who was she to ask questions, she hadn't the foggiest about their customs and every website she visited to learn about them were know-it-all windbags who have made up assumptions. So instead of opposing she hopped into the back of the carriage and sat down.

"So do you know the Lapps?" Duncan called over his shoulder as they made their way into the town.

"I...sort of, actually, I knew their daughter," she lied, she had no clue what their daughter was like. Just because Hannah Lapp gave birth to her, didn't exactly mean she knew her.

"I think you might have them mistaken for someone different, they only have a son, but Kendrick moved to Lancaster with his wife."

Well, this was a good start, she thought as she tucked her lip under her teeth, "Perhaps I am confused, but I suppose there is no harm in meeting them. Maybe they might know Hannah Lapp as extended family."

"Hannah Lapp," Duncan repeated, "The name sounds familiar."

The carriage came to a halt and Hayley fell forward along with her luggage and just then the heavens opened up.

"Come!" Duncan called and reached for a sheet to cover her luggage before effortlessly lifting her off the wagon and placing her on her feet, "The Lapp's live here. If you hurry I can wait and take you back to Richland Inn."

"Wait, what do you mean back to town, I need to be here in Ethridge," she protested as Duncan lead her up to the house where the Lapps lived.

"Well if the Lapps won't let you stay in their home, you have nowhere else to stay, unless you want to sleep in the barn."

"The barn?" she asked appalled.

"Duncan, vas in der velt?" an elderly man interrupted as he opened his door.

Duncan immediately removed his hat and clutched it in front of him then looked at her before turning his attention back to the older man.

"Mister Lapp, this is Hayley. She's come to Ethridge to look for..."

Before Duncan could continue Hayley stepped up and extended her hand, "Grandfather?"

The older man's complexion paled, and he exchanged looks with Duncan then looked at Hayley, "You're mistaken," he mumbled and moved to close the door, but then an elderly woman appeared and the expression on her face was one of pure shock.

"Hannah... you look just like her," she said in a trembling voice as her eyes shot full of tears.

"Grandmother?" Haylee said as she stood with her hands folded in front of her.

"Come, you're going to get soaking wet out in the rain," she said as she dragged Hayley into the house, despite her Grandfather's disapproval.

And as she disappeared into the kitchen she heard her grandfather mumble for Duncan to bring her luggage inside.

Her grandparents, she couldn't believe it. She was actually in the very house her biological mother grew up in. Her grandmother seemed far more accepting of her than her grandfather did, but she refused to make any assumptions until she had all the facts. For now, she will take the time she had to get to know them.

Chapter 3

A week since her arrival and all she could determine was that her mother, Hanna Lapp went on a Rumspringa and never returned.

"Did she never write to you?" Hayley asked her grandmother one morning after her grandfather left to go to work.

"She wrote to us, but only ever to let us know she was fine," her grandmother said softly as she continued with her sewing.

"But weren't you in the least bit worried?"

Mary put down her sewing and reached out for Hayley's hand, "Yah, we were worried, especially your grandfather, but our laws are different to those on the outside. Hannah made her choice and she had a chance to return."

Hayley sat quietly for a moment and squeezed her grandmother's hand. The short while she had been here in the Amish community of Ethridge, she had found a sense of peace and tranquillity she never felt before. With the exception of a minority of locals who walked wide circles around her, the younger people like her were friendly and very accommodating. She couldn't understand why her mother would have left for good, and trade this life for what lay outside in the world. But then, being on holiday in a strange place was far different that living the life in full.

A knock on the door drew her attention and her grandmother quickly set her sewing aside and went to open the door, and a few seconds later she returned with Duncan in tow.

"Hayley, Duncan is here to see you," her grandmother said smiling.

Duncan was another person she was growing fond of at an alarming rate, but thankfully the walls she erected around herself kept her level headed. She knew that the only reason she felt closer to him than any of the others was that he was the first person she met when she arrived.

"Hi Duncan, what a nice surprise," she said standing up.

"Good day to you Hayley," he nodded tucking his thumbs in his suspenders, "I was wondering if you would like to go to the market today, I have a few errands to run."

Hayley felt the slight flutter of butterflies in her stomach and tugged her hand into her midriff. It would be rather nice to get out a little and get to know other parts of the community, she thought and then nodded.

"It would be lovely, let me get my coat and purse," she said and hurried to her room.

She forced herself not to eavesdrop on her grandmother' and Duncan's conversation and quickly got what she needed before joining them.

In no time they were on the carriage and on their way to the market, this time Hayley got to sit in the front and not like some baggage on the back.

"So how are you enjoying your stay here in Ethridge?" Duncan asked curiously.

"It's nice. I mean, it's very different to city life, but so far I'm enjoying the peace and quiet," she said and glanced out over the landscape.

"Yah, it's very quiet. So did you manage to find out about Hannah?"

"A little," she said.

She didn't want to put the Lapps in any sort of disrepute, but she found it hard to believe that Duncan had no clue about her, but then again, he was probably still a baby when Hannah left the Amish community.

"So will you be moving on then?" he said clearing his throat.

Hayley turned to look at him and smiled, "Not sure, maybe. Tell me about this Rumspringa thing."

Duncan laughed and looked at her, "Well, Rumspringa means to run around, when the youngsters turn sixteen they can choose to go out and experience things outside of our community. It's each one's choice, some do it and some don't."

"Did you ever, I mean did you do it when you turned sixteen?" she asked curiously.

"Nay, I never did. I have all I need right here."

"So you never wonder what lies out in the cities."

Duncan drew the carriage to a halt and then turned to look at Hayley, studying her with those intense willow green eyes.

"Most young men leave because they are not satisfied with their life here, mostly because they are tempted by the modern world, and women," he said, his cheeks growing rosy.

Hayley tried to hide her smile and coughed softly, "So you never wanted to go find some hanky-panky?"

"Hanky -panky?" Duncan asked and blinked, "What is that?"

"Uh... well meeting women, dating and so on."

Duncan threw his head back and laughed, "Oh no, I had no interest in those things. Not then anyway," he said and then tugged on the reins sending the horse back onto the road, "I always believed that at the right time God will send the right woman my way. I'm a patient man Hayley Jones."

When he looked at her then, she felt her heart flutter in her chest and she immediately looked the other way. Her mind was clearly playing tricks on her; there was no way that Duncan would even consider looking at her twice. She was an outsider for one, and secondly, she wasn't exactly a virgin either. And although she still knew very little about their laws and traditions, she was sure the Amish probably had the highest moral values in the world second to nuns.

The rest of their trip was in silence, and a few miles further they finally reached the Amish Country Mall. Hayley was quite surprised by the variety of goods that were sold at this place, but more so how many non-Amish visited the place. It was a tourist distraction for curious people. And as she stood next to Duncan and the Carriage in her own authentic Amish dress, a sense of pride washed over her. Surprised that she actually felt Amish in some far-fetched way, she smiled at Duncan and then headed into the shop. She found it quite amusing that it was called a Mall when all it really had were old antique trinkets and a limited menu of food. There were some items for sale but it was hardly considered anything close to a shopping mall. When she exited the store she found Duncan standing next to her grandfather, both in deep conversation. Instead of barging in on them she took a walk around the store to give them their own time. Her grandfather had hardly spoken a word to her since her arrival and he was still a great big mystery to her. On occasion when she did ask her gran about him, she simply avoided the topic. She wasn't any closer to find out exactly why her mother never came back.

Chapter 4

Duncan couldn't help but admire Hayley, and although she was an outsider, she seemed to adapt quite well to the Amish life. It's been two weeks since he met her, and the more time he spent with her the more he started to like her. The first day he saw her was the first time he ever really looked at a woman. She was modestly dressed in a floral print dress that flowed elegantly down her body to her calves, but what intrigued him most was her shyness. The fact that he had the impulsive need to run his fingers through her long brown tresses was abnormal for him and he quickly stifled that need, by reminding himself that she was an outsider, which helped.

Normally when outsiders visited the Amish communities they stuck to their modern clothes, where the women wore as little as possible. No wonder so many of the Amish boys opted to go on their expedition to the cities, being tempted by the promises that the modern world presented. Two of his own best friends went out to experience the world and all it had to offer, but he never felt that desire or pull to know what happens out there. He was more than content to live this life of simplicity, working on the farm and making goat's cheese. There were many times when he attended the sings and where he contemplated the option of taking a wife, but none of the girls here in Ethridge ever made him feel the way he did now. And he was adamant that if he was going to take a wife, it would be someone who would completely consume his thoughts. He wanted the same love with a wife than his mother and father shared. He had never seen them argue, and they always showed their affection towards each other. And if they could have such a devoted marriage, why could he not have the same?

Duncan was caught in his own thoughts when the smell of burning wood and grass wafted through the air.

"Duncan!" It was Hayley who rode towards him on one of the Lapp's horses, her eyes wide, "Come quick, my grandfather's barn is on fire!" she cried.

In an instant, Duncan had called his father and his neighbors, and everyone else he could alert and they were on their way by carriage to the Lapp's farmlands. Up ahead he could see the plume of fire explode into the gray sky. Flames rolled outwards and embers were flying up into the sky.

When he pulled up next to Hayley where she dismounted the horse, he took the reins and handed it to another young man, "Take the horse to my father's barn and keep it there," he instructed and then turned to Hayley, "What happened?"

"I have no idea, we were all having dinner when we heard the loud crash of lightning, and not long after that the smoke was everywhere," she said ringing her hands together.

Duncan's concern for Hayley had to be set aside, and although he wanted to comfort her, he had to attend to the bigger problem.

"Okay, go to the house and stay inside," he ordered as he scooped a bucket of water from the trough.

"But I can help," she protested and reached for a small barrel.

"You've done enough, now go and sit with your grandmother, I'm sure she could use the company."

Her mouth opened in protest but then shut, and with a slight nod, she ran across the field towards the house.

They fought all night to get the fire under control, thankfully the Lord had blessed them with rain to help put the fire out, but all that was left were the charred remains of the barn in the smoky morning air that reeked of burnt wood and straw. His father had warned Fredrick about the tall dead tree that stood so close to the barn. But misfortune led to lighting striking the dead tree and causing it to fall on to the barn. Luckily it was only the barn that burned down, somehow the horses were freed before the barn was completely on fire, and he has the slightest suspicion that it was Hayley's quick thinking that saved the animals. As for the equipment, it was all replaceable.

"Thank you, son, if you didn't arrive when you did I would have lost all my horses," Mr. Lapp said as he came to stand next to Duncan.

"Nay, that was not my doing. Hayley saved the horses," he said and looked at the older man.

"Hayley saved them?" he asked disbelievingly.

"Yah, she came to fetch me on horseback, I've never seen a woman ride so well, but she came to call me straight away. By the time I got here the horses were already in the fields and Kent took them to my barn."

Fredrick stood quietly for a while rubbing his chin, and Duncan knew that he had his own demons to face. He too had never heard of Hannah Lapp, but spending time with Hayley he had learned a great deal.

"She's seeking your approval," Duncan said crossing his arms as both of them looked at what remained of the barn, "She deserves a fair chance."

"You're right," Fredrick said and then headed towards the house.

Duncan looked as the older man walked away, his shoulders hunched as if he carried a heavy burden, but he knew Hayley deserved a fair chance, she had nothing to do with her mother's disobedience or her choice to give her up for adoption.

Later that day, Duncan stood in his father's barn, grooming the Lapps' horses. The least he could do was make sure that none of them were injured. But more than anything he needed to keep busy so that he could chase the thoughts of Hayley from his mind. Every waking hour was seemingly consumed by thoughts of her, and after her courageous act it was even worse. Now he knew exactly how King Solomon must have felt, being tempted by a beautiful woman.

"Duncan?" he heard Hayley's voice from outside the barn.

"In here!" he answered and tossed the brush in the sack hanging on the wall.

"Oh there you are," she said smiling and held out a basket for him, "Grandma and I baked these to thank you for helping us out with the horses."

Duncan smiled and took the basket filled with cookies, "Thanks, but I think you deserve all the credit, if it wasn't for you these horses would be charred with the barn."

He noticed Hayley blush as she averted her eyes, "I love horses, I had to do something."

Duncan stepped closer and reached out to tuck his finger under her chin, "And you did an amazing job of saving them," he said but his voice betrayed him.

This close to her, he could smell the fresh scent of lavender and vanilla, and although it was just the crook of his finger brushing her unblemished skin under her chin, it was the silk soft smoothness that tempted him more than anything. And without a second thought, he stepped in and pressed his lips against hers. Hers were soft, like cotton pillows and although the kiss was brief, it was a defying moment for him. He knew there and then that Hayley was the woman he'd been waiting for all these years.

He broke the chaste kiss but didn't step away from her; instead he kept his eyes locked on hers. It was that moment between two people where words were irrelevant syllables and consonants were fleeting sounds that would never be able to express the emotions that sparked between them.

It was Hayley that stepped away first, and how shyly tucked a strand of hair behind her ear.

"My grandfather said that they will be doing a barn rising this coming weekend, will you come?" she asked softly.

"I wouldn't miss it for the world," Duncan said.

And as Hayley walked back out of the Barn she looked back over at him again and smiled.

Duncan felt like a teenager for the first time, and now more than ever was he determined to make Hayley Jones his wife.

Chapter 5

The barn raising was well on its way, the men from the community had spent most of the morning working and Hayley was amazed by how quickly the barn started taking shape. She heard many stories about this experience and how the Amish are able to build an entire barn in one day, but she had never seen it with her own eyes. Duncan was at the front line of everything. He did the planning and the design, his skill as a builder came in handy and it appeared that young to old admired him, but not nearly as much as she did.

When she first decided to come to Ethridge, finding love was the last thing she anticipated. After her failed engagement to Jase, she had sworn off on ever dating again, but here she was, utterly captivated by Duncan. He was the complete opposite to Jase. He was kind, considerate, a true gentleman and there was something about him that she craved.

"He's a fine young man," her gran said as she handed her the basket of fresh fruit.

Hayley tore her eyes away from the barn and smiled at her gran, "Yes, he is," she admitted.

"You know, Hannah never told us about you until after she gave you up for adoption," her grandmother started, "When she told us your grandfather begged her to withdraw the adoption and rather send you to us."

Hayley sat down opposite her gran at the wooden table, "So you did know about me?"

"Oh yes we did, but your mother had already handed you to your new parents, and we had no way of finding you. That day you arrived here in Ethridge, you were a spitting image of my Hannah."

Hayley's eyes shot full of tears and she reached out to take her grandmother's hand, "My adopted parents were good people, they really looked after me as if I was their own."

"I know, but I can't help wonder just how things would have been if Hannah had come back home," the older woman admitted and lowered her eyes.

"I'm here now though, and you've made me feel at home."

"Yah, yah, I know. I've been trying my best. Your grandfather blames himself for what happened, but he's a good man."

Hayley smiled and then looked back at the men toiling in the sun. Her grandfather was a proud but humble man, and she knew that deep down he cared for her.

By six o'clock that evening, the barn stood tall in all its glory. Brand spanking new as if no disaster had struck it just a week ago, and everyone in the community had gathered to celebrate the event. It was a festive atmosphere and for the first time in her life Hayley felt as if she belonged. Over the weeks she spent here in Ethridge learning to bake and quilt, she hardly thought of her life in the city. And the hustle and bustle of peak hour traffic and busy shopping malls were nothing but a distant memory of a temporary life she once knew.

She made a few friends and even the older people had started to like her. Maybe it was due to the fact that she did not come here to dispute their faith or their ways, but she embraced it like any Amish citizen would.

From across the group of people, she caught Duncan looking at her. But instead of looking away, she smiled at him, and even when one of his friends tapped him on his shoulder he still looked her way, refusing to drop his glance. The sight of him made her knees weak. She had to force herself to look away before her grandfather came to sit beside her.

"My dear," he started sounding uncomfortable, "I owe you an apology for my behavior."

Hayley turned to her grandfather and smiled, "No need, you had a lot to cope with, with my untimely arrival. I should have taken better care to notify you before I just dropped in."

"No, it's not that. I-I never gave your mother a chance to rectify things and for that, I am forever guilty, I should have gone to find her."

Fredrick pinched the bridge of his nose and shut his eyes and Hayley knew he was fighting back the tears, she gently placed her hand on his, "The choices we make are our own, and we are all responsible for them, no one can take responsibility for the mistakes of others."

There was a moment of silence, and when her grandfather looked up at her again he smiled tenderly, "You will make a wonderful Amish woman," he said and patted her hand, "And Duncan would choose well to ask for your hand."

"Hayley, come!" One of the girls called and tugged her up by her hand, "You must join in on the sing."

Before Hayley could process the words of her grandfather she was caught smack bang in the middle with a bunch of the younger people, and although there were no instruments, the clapping of hands and the harmonies of voices made the songs come to life. Among the crowd was Duncan, subtly making his way closer to her and the closer he came the more her heart beat out of control and the butterflies that hijacked her insides fluttered up a storm. She might very well be an outsider but she could not deny the fact that somehow Providence had claimed a victory.

"Would you spare me a few minutes of your time?" Duncan whispered as he reached her.

"Of course," she said and followed him outside.

Duncan had his hands tucked in his pockets as he stood outside. The moonlight spilled down from the heavens like a silver curtain, bathing their surroundings in silver dust and casting its subtle glow over them. And as Hayley came to stand next to him, they both glanced up at the sky.

"Hayley..."

"Duncan..."

They started at the same time and then burst out laughing.

"You first," Hayley insisted and Duncan smiled and turned towards her.

"Okay, well, I'm sure this will come as no surprise to you, but I thought it best I clear the air," he started clutching his hand in his hands, "I think or rather, I know that I have grown very fond of you, and I know that it may be a little more complicated than usual, but I have spoken to your grandfather."

Hayley stood playing with the string of her prayer cap, coiling it around her index finger nervously. It felt as if her heart was going to jump out of her throat as Duncan went on, explaining how he had asked her grandfather if he would allow him to court her. A few weeks ago, she would never have considered this, but now where she stood under the moonlit sky, with her hand in Duncan's she knew exactly what she wanted.

"And did my grandfather approve?" she asked curiously biting her lip.

"He did indeed, which is why I have gathered to courage to ask you in person," he admitted and smiled.

Hayley shifted her weight and sucked in a breath, she had no idea how Amish dating customs worked. Of all the things she had yet to learn, dating hardly featured and she recalled only briefly spot reading over that section.

"So are we going to be bundling?" she asked innocently and blushed.

Duncan raised his brows and chuckled, "My dear Hayley, you have so much to learn still, no one does that anymore," he said and stepped closer to her and reached to remove her prayer cap.

"Is that allowed?" She whispered softly as Duncan's lips hovered over hers and he pulled the pin that secured her hair in a bun lose.

"What happens between us, and the Lord, is all that matters," he said and then wrapped her loose braid around his hand and kissed her fully on the lips.

Chapter 6

Hayley stood in front of the mirror, while her grandmother fussed with her long hair. It's been a year since she joined the community and although her and Duncan's feelings for each other were no secret to the rest of the community, they both kept their word to follow the rules and customs as required by the Amish Council.

"So the food is almost ready. Once your Grandfather and I are off to the church service, you and Duncan can sit down and celebrate your betrothal."

Hayley looked in the reflection of the mirror at her grandmother, the woman she had grown to love and smiled, "Do you think I will make him happy, Grossmammi?" she asked.

"Natuurlijk! You're his future and the woman he had been waiting for all this time," her gran reassured her.

After her grandparents left to go to church, where the minister would be announcing the brides to be, she waited patiently at the house for Duncan to arrive. She kept looking at the clock on the wall, it was a unique hand crafted clock made especially for her by Duncan, as a courtship gift. Time seemed like it had deliberately slowed down, and when she heard the carriage finally pull up in front of the house, she had to force herself to stay calm and not rush into his arms. Other than the first time he kissed her, and the second and the third, this was probably one of the most amazing moments in her life. After tonight, she would officially be engaged, and by October, only two months away, she would be Mrs. Hayley Beiler.

"You do know that you still have a choice right?" Duncan said much later after they had finished dessert.

"I have made my choice, and it is to stay here with you," she said smiling.

They were seated on a wooden bench outside on the porch; waiting for the Lapp's to arrive.

"Are you a hundred percent sure?" he asked again, this time lacing his fingers with hers.

Hayley turned to him and placed her free hand over their entwined fingers. The past few months she had made the effort to learn their various customs, do bible study, get familiar with their laws, but she knew beyond anything that her life was here with him.

"Duncan, I am happy and I would not change this for anything," she said and then leaned close enough for her lips to brush his, "Ich liebe dich," she whispered and gave him a chaste kiss on his lips.

"And I love you, Hayley Jones," Duncan said, smiling from ear to ear and then quoted Songs of Solomon, "You are altogether beautiful, my darling, beautiful in every way."

~*~

*Most of all, let love guide your way.* Col 3:14